The City in the Stars

TOM SWIFT ®
THE CITY IN THE STARS
VICTOR APPLETON

WANDERER BOOKS
Published by Simon & Schuster, New York

Published by WANDERER BOOKS
A Simon & Schuster Division of
Gulf & Western Corporation
Simon & Schuster Building
1230 Avenue of the Americas
New York, New York 10020

Manufactured in the United States of America
10 9 8 7 6 5 4 3 2 1
WANDERER and colophon are trademarks
of Simon & Schuster
TOM SWIFT is a trademark of Stratemeyer Syndicate, registered in
the United States Patent and Trademark Office
Library of Congress Cataloging in Publication Data
Appleton, Victor, pseud.
The city in the stars.
(Tom Swift; 1)
SUMMARY: Despite attempts to sabotage his newly invented fusion
drive spacecraft, a young scientist investigates the sinister, eminent head
of the space colony who is hiding serious flaws in his own new craft.
[1. Science fiction] I. Title.
PZ7.A652Ci   [Fic]   80-27001
ISBN 0-671-41120-9
ISBN 0-671-41115-2 (pbk.)

CONTENTS

Chapter One

Something was wrong, really wrong.

The void of space was no place for anything to go wrong, but Tom Swift's small racing ship was in deep trouble.

The explosion had been soundless. He had felt it through the frame and seen the flash of light reflected off his instrument panel. The huge cylinder of the distant space colony *New America* had seemed to buck and veer as Tom's vessel went out of control.

Tom twisted in his seat, looking through the tough plastic of his spacesuit helmet at the twisted wreckage behind him. The guidance mechanism of his prototype racing ship was a mess and he couldn't shut off the supply of fuel to the flaring rocket.

7

New America was receding. Beyond it the big blue marble of Earth was also perceptively dwindling and Tom Swift was shooting into space, out of control.

"I'm having some problems here, Ben," Tom said. He kept his voice calm as he spoke to the computer technician monitoring his test flight.

"Red alert," Ben Walking Eagle responded. "Gotcha on the screens, Tom, and it doesn't look good. Nothing stable. Your readings are all over the map. Switching to visual."

There was a quick flow of information across Tom's readout screens as he checked his ship's condition. Tiny silicon chips planted all over the ship's life support system and engineering complex told their story.

"You're tumbling," Ben said, the tension in his voice evident. "You're going out of the test field . . ." He paused. "Toward . . . uh . . . the Sun."

"I've got ninety-two million miles yet. I'll be dead of starvation long before I heat up."

"Tom, there's no rescue tug available right now. They're taking care of the ore shipment coming up from the Moon, and . . ." He stopped and Tom frowned.

"You mean, I . . ." Tom's throat tightened in fear. "This ship's coming apart, Ben, and—"

A shudder almost threw him from the bucket seat in the cramped cockpit. Looking around, he saw most of the steering mechanism rip loose, white with heat from the flaring jet. The fragment spun over Tom's head and disappeared from his sight.

"Ben! A piece came off. Check it, quickly!"

"Got it on radar," the computer technician replied. "Feeding it to the computer now and . . . uh-oh!"

"What is it?" Tom asked.

"Heading toward us." Tom could hear Ben speaking to others in the distant control center, warning of the hot fragment in short trajectory toward *New America*.

Tom checked his air supply, thankful that he had thought to wear a full spacesuit, with a four-hour tank of air, and to bring an extra two-hour bottle of breathing mixture. Half of his controls were useless, frozen by the explosion, and beyond repair. If he had to wait for rescue to come from *New America*, at least he would have air.

"Computer says we're on collision paths," Ben said over the radio. "I've alerted the damage control teams. Just sit tight, buddy. We're trying to get it together here."

Tom sighed. Inaction was frustrating to him. He rechecked his air supply and once again tried to unfreeze the controls, but the mechanism was definitely broken.

The vast cylinder that was *New America* seemed

to rotate around him, gradually shrinking as Tom sped away toward the Sun. The three-mile-long colony was a mile in diameter and spun on its long axis, creating a gravity nine-tenths that of Earth's for the fifty thousand inhabitants within its metal shell. The artificial gravity held farms, streams of purest water, a small lake, and decorative forests with dwellings nestled among the trees on the inside of the rotating cylinder. Somehow, Tom never quite got used to water being stuck to the "ceiling"; if he walked "up" the gentle curving side of the colony, he'd get to the lake and the forests would then be under his feet.

The entire concept of a city in space was exciting to him. As the son of Mr. Tom Swift, head of Swift Enterprises and the designing contractor for *New America*, Tom knew firsthand that the engineering challenges had been tremendous. He was proud that he had been able to make some modest contributions toward the design of the giant space colony, but he was in awe of the work that had been necessary to make the project a reality.

And now, there were industries. Perfect ball bearings were made in space, where gravity did not distort their spherical perfection. Long crystals were grown to make extraordinarily strong materials. Medicine had profited too, for certain viruses were synthesized far more expertly in the relatively "clean environment." There were a hundred experiments going on. Outer space was a growth industry, and Swift Enterprises was a vital part of it.

Tom was a part of it, too, for he had inherited his father's inventive genius and inquisitive mind, as well as his big-boned, six-foot frame and sandy-blond hair. At eighteen, Tom was already an important and active contributor to the family business, the giant multimillion-dollar scientific-industrial complex known as Swift Enterprises. From its main site on the outskirts of Shopton, New Mexico, the company extended its concerns all over the world, and its vast and varied interests provided constant challenges for the young man.

Farther along in orbit, another space colony called *Sunflower* was in the early stages of construction. It had a different design from *New America*, being a torus-shaped structure that looked something like an inner tube. Both were located at points where the Earth's gravity and the Moon's gravity cancel each other out, so they could stay there forever, relatively unassisted.

Like *New America*, *Sunflower* had mirrors that collected sunlight, and large multipaned windows to admit it. A day-and-night cycle was simulated by redirecting the mirrors at scheduled hours.

But unlike *New America*, it did not have a chunk of hot metal shooting toward it.

Tom groaned in frustration. There must be something he could do. Once again, he reviewed his options.

He could unbuckle and literally leap from the tumbling ship, hoping to drift toward *New America*. But did he have enough air? And could he correctly gauge the jump from a ship out of control?

Or he could stay put and wait. But it wasn't in him to just sit!

Every second of inaction was taking him farther away from *New America* and closer to the Sun. He came to a decision and punched the transmit button on his suit radio.

"I'm abandoning the ship, Ben," he said. Without waiting for a reply, he unbuckled the safety harness and floated free of the padded seat. He was calm now; the decision to take action had erased his doubts and fears.

"I'm in no position to talk you out of it, Tom," Ben broke in. "It's crazy down here. Everybody's running to his emergency station and I can't seem to locate Doctor Grotz. He's the only one who can authorize a rescue tug. Do one thing for me, though. Turn on your suit transponder. That way, at least I'll know where you are!"

Tom reached up and pressed the tiny button located on his helmet, just above his forehead.

"I'm getting a strong signal," Ben said almost immediately. "Good luck."

Tom took one last look around the ship. Was there anything he could salvage from it that might aid him once he was outside? There was the auxiliary bottle of breathing mixture—a two-hour buffer between him and disaster. He took it out of its restraining harness and strapped it onto his suit's backpack before reaching up and switching off the cockpit's interior lights. It was a useless gesture, but it was habit. Then he began the slow, weightless crawl to the hatch.

Tom felt no regret at leaving the ship. He had been plagued by problems from the beginning. Every time something had happened he wondered where he had gone wrong, but he had always come up with a blank. The Prometheus drive should have worked. It had been tested thoroughly by its inventor, Dr. Hans Grotz, now the acting director of *New America*. This drive should have made Tom's small ship the fastest one in its class. Had he made a mistake in the interpretation of Grotz's design? It had annoyed him that he just couldn't pin the malfunctions down, and he had transferred that annoyance to the small ship. That's why it had always been just a ship to him.

Holding on to the safety handle with one hand, Tom unlocked the hatch. He felt, rather than heard, the small pop of the door seal, and then he was staring at black, open space as the hatch door slid open on its pneumatic hinges. The ship was tumbling slowly clockwise. *New America* came into view in the distance.

Tom knew that his most immediate problem was to jump clear of the ship so that any projections on the hull wouldn't knock him unconscious or propel him in the wrong direction. He would have to use the tumbling of the ship itself to accomplish this.

"Thousand and one, thousand and two, thousand and three . . ." Tom timed a revolution of the ship from the time *New America* left his view until it reappeared. Seventy seconds. He mentally calculated the curve of his jump based on that time. It was just like figuring the trajectory of a baseball back on Earth. *New America* was the catcher in this game, the ship was the pitcher, and Tom was the ball. If he missed, though, he would lose more than just a baseball game.

"Thousand thirty, thousand thirty-one, out!" Still holding on to the safety handle, Tom pulled himself out of the ship. He was floating in space connected to the ship by only one hand.

"Thousand forty, thousand forty-one, thousand forty-two . . ." He continued to count under his breath as the ship dragged him upward.

"Thousand fifty-nine, thousand sixty, go!" It took all of Tom's willpower to let go of the safety handle when every instinct screamed at him to hang on. The ship was solid. It was real. It was security. Space was ... nothingness! But Tom's reason willed the muscles of his fingers to let go.

There was no feeling of motion, but Tom saw that he was moving away from the ship in a lazy, tumbling arc. The only sound was his own breath echoing in his helmet.

Now, the never-ending vastness of space began to bear down on him like a great weight. He swallowed hard and focused his attention on his immediate problem.

Tom was moving toward *New America,* but he was also tumbling head over heels as a result of having used the ship to launch his escape. He knew he had to stop the tumbling somehow. He needed a force to counter the direction of his tumble, a release of something under pressure. A jet of air from the extra bottle of breathing mixture would do the trick. Could he afford to use it that way?

The air-level indicator in his helmet was green, which meant he had enough air for a while. How long would it be before he needed his extra tank? He had been on suit air the whole test period, and he had been up three and a half hours. That left approximately a half hour's worth of air. Would the rescue tug get to him within that time?

When he was growing up, Tom had listened wide-eyed to the stories that his father's senior pilots liked to tell about their adventures in space. They had all agreed on one thing: if you ran out of air in space, you were finished. Many of them had talked about their frustration and rage when they maintained radio contact with stranded friends to the end, listening and not being able to help. What would it be like to suffocate alone, drifting in space?

Tom shook himself. He had no time to think about that. He had to act. The decision to abandon ship had been his own. If he was going to lose his life, it would be better to die knowing he had tried to save himself than to sit and wait for death.

Tom unhooked the auxiliary airtank from his suit and looked at the connection. It was a simple spring-loaded air valve like the ones on his bicycle tires. He held the tank in his arms, as tightly as he could, and pressed the center of the valve.

He could neither see nor hear the air hissing out of the bottle, but he felt its vibration through his suit. His head-over-heels tumbling slowed.

He pressed the valve again, letting out more of the precious breathing mixture, and it slowed even more. Now, he could get his bearings. He looked for *New America,* and an invisible hand of ice gripped his stomach. He was no longer heading in a straight line toward the station! The blasts of pressurized air had stopped his tumbling all right, but they had also pushed him out of line with *New America*. To make matters worse, his air-level indicator flipped from green to orange. He only had fifteen minutes of suit air left!

Chapter Two

"I won't authorize it, Ben! Every one of those tugs is on an important assignment and—"

"But Doctor Grotz," Ben interrupted, impatiently.

"Mister Swift knew the risk he was taking when he went out on that test flight . . ."

"But—"

". . . and now, because of his carelessness and stupidity, the safety of this entire station and its personnel is in jeopardy. He'll just have to wait. I only hope for his sake, he can!"

Benjamin Franklin Walking Eagle looked straight into the steel-gray eyes of Dr. Hans Grotz. He tried to keep the level of his voice respectful, but inside, he was boiling mad.

18

"Doctor Grotz, we are talking about a man who is stranded in space, not some abstract mathematical concept. How much difference can it make in your schedule to divert one tug to rescue him?"

As soon as the alert had been sounded, the monitoring room had become jammed with technicians. The noise level had risen sharply as the technicians monitored the fragment of Tom's ship on the various pieces of equipment in the small room. But now as Ben and Dr. Grotz argued, there was a tense silence, punctuated only by the whirs, clicks, and beeps of the machines.

"I'm not going to debate the point any longer, Ben. I've got an emergency to handle!"

"Okay, Doctor Grotz," said Ben, deadly calm now. "Are you going to be the one to tell Tom we're not coming out to pick him up? Here! Take the mike. I want to see how you tell someone that you're going to let him die!"

Dr. Grotz looked at Ben, his face impassive. "No. That's your job, Ben, I'm sure you'll handle it with your usual competence." Ben was stunned into silence, and he watched the big man turn and crisply walk to the telemeter. Grotz seemed to become engrossed as a technician traced for him the path of the piece of debris from Tom's ship. Then, he left the monitoring room.

In the hall outside, people scurried to get out

of Grotz's path as the director passed. Grotz did not alter his stride to avoid them. He never did.

Grotz was walking briskly, but without any sense of immediate danger. When he entered his office, he was calm inside, for he knew that at least he was safe and in the end, he was all that mattered. He was the center of everything—the hub around which the life of *New America* revolved. The trajectory of the plummeting piece of debris had been plotted, and this area was in no danger. He had made sure of that before leaving the monitoring room.

Young Swift. Now there was a problem—something he had no control over, something that refused to fit in with the well-ordered society he had created in *New America* since a random stroke of luck had left him in charge months ago. The permanent director of the colony had had a heart attack—from the pressures, it was said—and Grotz had been more than happy to step in until a new director was found. No one was in a hurry to find one, however, so Grotz continued to exploit the convenient power base the position offered. If young Swift refused to march in step with the rest of his well-ordered citizenry of *New America*, he would have to be eliminated. Grotz chuckled to himself softly. He *was* being eliminated—by his own devices.

Grotz punched his intercom and his secretary's

voice responded immediately. He liked that. He demanded immediate service. "Wilma, have Worden and Deckert picked up their checks yet?"

"No, Doctor Grotz. I called both of them, but there was no answer. They've been spending a lot of time down at the hangar deck lately, working on their racer, the *Régine*."

"That infernal race. I swear this is going to be the last one. Be sure they see me when they come in."

Grotz reached into his desk and took out a small key. He swiveled around in his chair and inserted it into an unmarked slot in his personal computer console. Instantly, the screen came to life, and Grotz punched a sequence of numbers and then the key word "Bonaparte." The screen began to fill up rapidly with index headings and numbers. Chewing his lip in silence, Grotz looked at the display, just as he had looked at it a hundred times since the last series of stress tests on his Prometheus drive had been completed. Nothing had changed. The errors in his original calculations still stood out among the figures, taunting him—an unfortunate result of the rush to publish that was the bane of every prominent scientist. He did not regret the haste; the publication of his planetary drive had been timed to make him eligible for this year's Nobel Prize. What he regretted was that, of all the times he had fudged on test results to meet a deadline, this had to be the time that his guess was wrong. The Prometheus drive would fail; there was no doubt. He would have to correct the errors, then correct the stress test records— or he would have to look for someone else to blame.

A few miles outside *New America*, Tom Swift's air-level indicator flipped from orange to red. That was it for the big tank. Tom reached back and carefully unbuckled the holding strap across the middle of the tank. He took a deep breath and then pulled the release lever. Two metal tangs unlocked. Reaching back with his elbow, he shoved the tank out of its bracket and watched it float away. Normally, he would have reached around and grabbed the empty tank to take back to the ship for refilling. But he had no ship now, and the big tank would be an awkward nuisance. He took the auxiliary tank out of its harness and put it into place in the bracket. He locked the support tangs into place and took a breath. He now had less than two hours to get to safety.

Reaching down, he punched the transmit button on his suit radio. "Ben! What's the status of things down there?" Tom heard the crackling sound of radio static in his ear. He was getting interference from *New America* now. Ben came on a second later and Tom could tell that the young computer technician was upset.

"Um . . . the computer shows you're off course for *New America* . . . and . . . uh . . . I have some bad news for you. Doctor Grotz won't authorize a rescue tug for you. I don't know what else to say. He says he can't release them from their assignments."

Tom swallowed hard. "You . . . you don't have to say anything, Ben. I'm sure Doctor Grotz has his reasons. I'll just have to make it any way I can, that's all. I'm not far away from *New America*. All I really have to do is get back on a straight line with you and I'll get there eventually."

"I'll give you all the help I can from down here, buddy. I feel so . . . helpless right now!"

The momentum of his jump from the ship was still carrying Tom in the general direction of *New America*, but if he stayed on his present course, he would miss the station. The first thing he had to do, then, was get back on course. The trouble was that he only had one tank of air for both propulsion and breathing. Any air he used for propulsion was that much less for him to breathe! He took a deep breath and detached the tank from its bracket. Pointing the nozzle end so that the released air would shove him toward *New America*, he depressed the valve. As the air was released, Ben's voice cut in.

"I'm tracking you, Tom. You're moving back toward us now, but the computer says that at your present speed you'll overshoot us. What are you using for propulsion? Tom? Come in, Tom!"

Tom reattached his airtank and took a welcome breath of air.

"My air supply," he gasped. "Unfortunately, I can't tell how long to depress the air valve. I've got to be losing a lot of air each time I do it, and I'm wasting it because I can only estimate."

"Maybe I can—" Ben broke off abruptly and Tom could hear voices in the background. Then Ben spoke again.

"Thirty seconds to impact. That piece of your ship's coming home the hard way, and they say I've got to go. I'll be back when I can. Out."

Tom Swift knew he was really alone now. He took a series of deep breaths. Hyperventilating would store up a little more oxygen in his brain cells, and that might enable him to hold out just a few seconds longer. One long blast would send him toward the outside airlock located on the end of *New America*. It would probably use up the rest of the air in the tank as well. Even if he did it, he might not get there. If he didn't do it, he would definitely not get there. *Might not* seemed like the best choice.

Out of the corner of his eye, Tom saw a short,

bright flash of light. The piece of his ship had passed one of the solar mirrors girding the middle of the city in space, and the sunlight had been reflected off it momentarily. *New America* had been hit.

Now Tom was filled with a new sense of urgency. He couldn't guess at how much damage had been done, but it could be bad. He knew it was his responsibility to get back there and help. Holding on to the bottle, he pressed the air valve as far down as it would go.

As his speed increased, *New America* loomed larger and larger ahead until, finally, it filled his view totally. Using a series of short blasts of air, he maneuvered himself to where he could see the emergency airlock door at the end of the revolving cylinder. Opening that door would be his only chance to live.

The airlock had been used mainly during the construction of *New America* to enable the workers to get in and out of the structure easily. It could be worked by hand from the outside simply by emptying the pressure chamber and then turning the huge wheel that unlocked the door. It was still used when outside repairs had to be done by hand in that area, but since the completion of the colony, most traffic went in and out of *New America* from the other end. Tom hoped that the airlock would still be in usable condition.

Tom stopped his forward motion with a blast of air and floated in front of the door. He connected the air bottle one last time. He was going to try a straight run for the door. He needed one more blast of air to do it. Tom hoped he had enough left, but he couldn't even guess at how much he had used getting here.

Speed was also a factor. Tom didn't know how long he would be able to hold his breath. He would have to reach the door, empty the airlock, and open the door on the same breath.

"Here goes!" He pressed the air valve down as hard as he could. He felt the air rushing out, and he began to move rapidly toward the airlock door. Then, suddenly, the vibrations he had come to know as the sign that air was being released stopped.

The only air left now was that in his lungs and what might be in the suit. He flung the tank from him and reached out with his arms, bracing himself for impact with *New America.* He struck hard. Desperately, he grabbed for a handhold to keep from bouncing back out into space and found one on the huge hinge of the airlock door. Tom pulled himself down to the door and slammed his fist onto the button marked AIRLOCK CYCLE. Immediately, a red light began flashing over the door as the air was automatically drained from the chamber. This equalized the pressure of the chamber with that of space so that Tom could open the door. What seemed to Tom like an eternity later, the light flashed green. His lungs aching, he turned the wheel, unlocking the door. He was very weak by the time it opened, and with his last bit of strength, he pulled himself inside and locked it. He let his breath out then and quickly sucked in another. It was leftover suit air, mostly carbon dioxide, but it was all he had. He was getting dizzy as he punched the button marked PRESSURIZE. He lay floating in the chamber, not even aware of the reading on the pressure gauge. Tom began to black out!

Chapter Three

Just as Tom began to lose consciousness, he saw a light flash green. Desperately he tore off his helmet, gasping and gulping in air. He sank to the floor, too weak from the lack of oxygen to do anything but breathe. That was close, he said to himself. It was several minutes before he had the strength to leave the chamber.

"Get out of the way!"

Tom looked over his shoulder, then quickly slapped himself flat against the wall of the corridor. Three men in lightweight pressure suits hurried past him. The young inventor saw they were lugging a tank marked CONTENTS UNDER PRESSURE and striped with luminescent orange decals. Tom turned his head to watch them hurry down the narrow corridor and saw the words

EMERGENCY REPAIR stenciled on the backs of their suits.

"Hey, wait!" Tom shouted after them, but the men did not pause. He shoved off the wall and hurried after them, but they had disappeared at a junction of several passages.

The emergency airlock was behind him. Since he had never had to use it before, he was now in an area with which he was unfamiliar. He wanted to get to the place where the fragment of his ship had come through the huge window. He picked the passage most likely to get him there and began walking slowly, hindered by the awkward spacesuit he was still wearing.

Halting momentarily, Tom bent over and switched off his magnetic boots. As handy as they were in space, providing a sort of pseudogravity, they were a great hindrance inside. He did not want to take the time to divest himself of the bulky suit, so he clumped along as rapidly as he could.

The corridor twisted and turned, branched and merged. He heard muffled shouts ahead of him, but he couldn't quite seem to catch up. He met no one in the antiseptically clean passages from whom he could ask directions.

Tom was puffing with exertion when a pressure hatch came into sight at the end of the corridor. He knew that the skin of the huge colony was actually double, with a thickness of storage rooms, experimental labs, and tanks sandwiched between the inner and outer surfaces. The hatch before him was heavy, ribbed with welded steel, and set into a sturdy wall of honeycomb metal of great strength.

The locking mechanism was simple and operated manually by turning a wheel. And the wheel was spinning shut, locking it.

Tom threw himself against the hatch, striking it with the edge of his balled fist. "Stop! Wait!" He heard a muffled exclamation from the other side, then the wheel reversed itself. The hatch popped open with a soft sound, and Tom squeezed through. He was inside the colony itself.

The vast cylinder stretched away from him for three miles, a green, blue, and brown carpet covering its inside surface. He was only vaguely aware of the lake sparkling above him. He saw the long, unbroken strips of window, hundreds of feet wide and thousands of feet long, that stretched along the surface. Some of the transparent windows showed the blackness of space, while others glowed softly with the light reflected in from the Sun by the huge outside mirrors.

Tom could see bits of paper and swirls of dust moving toward one strip. The break. The air was leaking out, expelled by the interior pressure.

The puncture was below Tom's present position, and he started to climb down the slope from the curved end toward the flatlands of the central cylinder.

"Hey, young fella, wait a minute." The man behind the hatch was waving at Tom.

"Which way is the best way to the break?" the young inventor asked. The end of the cylinder was something of a wilderness region, with piles of rock from the Moon, some dirt, and a few plantings of pines and bushes.

"Hold on," the old man said. He looked at Tom closely. "Wait a minute, you're the Swift boy, aren't you?"

"Yes. Is that the way, down past that grove? Or should I circle over by those rocks and go down that path?"

"How'd you get back, boy? We heard you were heading out to the Sun."

"Please, sir, I'll tell you all about that later. I want to go help!" Tom pointed at the repair crews he could see working on the rupture.

"We all felt terrible," the man said. "How did it happen?"

"Please!" Tom said. "Which way?"

The man waved a hand negligently. "Aw, they'll take care of it. That's their job. Don't worry too much about the air. It's just a little hole. Take *weeks* to leak everything out a hole as teeny as that one."

"I can't help it. My ship's responsible for that.

I've got to go help. Now which way is quickest?"

"That way." The man shrugged, and Tom clumped off as quickly as he could. The path led down through the small pines, and the gravity increased with every step. As he got closer to the flatlands, he was moving even slower. He passed more houses, all of them built of the lightest materials, for they were nothing more than privacy shields. There were no winds or storms within the colony, and rain was artificially created, usually during the sleep cycle. Each house had its own small garden, and the predominant theme was Japanese, with the precise, artistic, and somewhat miniaturized attitude of the Oriental toward his environment.

But the beauty and cleanliness of *New America* were not what interested Tom Swift just then. For a moment, he lost sight of the ruptured section behind the trees and houses. Then he turned a corner in the path that had become a meandering lane and saw the long window before him.

Like immense slots, the windows pierced the skin of *New America,* letting in the life-giving sunlight. The windows were composed of large, transparent, hexagonal plates made of an immensely strong plastic. Each of these barely discernible plates was composed of hundreds of smaller hexagons bonded together. The principle was based on an idea of Tom's father;

if a window was breached—by a meteorite coming in, or something falling out—the small hexagons would shatter like safety glass, leaving a smaller hole with straight edges, rather than a larger, jagged hole. This would make for faster and easier repair.

Tom didn't know whether the hole was big or little by colony standards. He only knew that it was a hole he had made. The fact that he'd made it indirectly, and by accident, didn't matter. He was responsible.

He hurried forward, right up to the chest-high wall that surrounded the great slot of a window. Tom saw a bird fluttering overhead, struggling in the unaccustomed breeze. It beat its way clear and grasped the limb of a nearby pine.

Tom moved quickly along the wall to the open repair gate, where he was stopped by a young man in an orange pressure suit. "Whoa! No civilians allowed out there."

"But it's my fault. I want to help."

"*Uh-uh.*" The man did not even look at Tom. He was watching the crews getting into position.

It was tricky out there on the smooth surface. Now that he was closer, Tom could see that every hundred feet or so there was a metal strut that snaked its way through the hexagons as added reinforcement. It was along these struts that most of the repair crews were moving. Tom saw them unfold a bulky, transparent bag of some sort and snap it to another similar bag. Then these two were joined to a third and fourth. All the time the dust was visible, streaming through into space.

"Excuse me," the repairman said, shouldering Tom aside. Tom saw that a transparent hose snaked from a tank lying by the wall, out across the plastic window. Someone out there was connecting it to the linked bags. The tank was the one Tom had seen carried by the emergency repair crew. The crewman turned the valve, and there was a hissing sound.

Through the transparent hose, Tom could see a milky liquid coursing along. It flowed into the bags, and at once began to expand to several times its volume. Tom saw other hoses connected to other bags, filling them with the rapidly expanding foam. The bags became rigid as the foam set, forming into large hexagons. Seven of them linked together formed a patch much larger than the hole. The repair crew would maneuver the patch over the hole and, with the air pressure holding it in place, seal it down. The exterior repair crews could take their time about replacing the immense panes.

Just as they were about to pick up the patch, there was a ripping sound. Another section of the window broke loose and fell away. The breeze became a wind. A bird tumbled past Tom and went flapping into space. The repair crew clung to the patch as it tried to flip up, caught by the sudden gust.

The crewman next to Tom snapped his helmet into place and gestured for Tom to follow suit. But Tom had no air left in his tank. He was gasping for breath and squinting against the swirl of dust. He saw a crewman rise and plant his suction shoes against the slick plastic surface, then fall, pushed roughly by the wind.

It was a gale now, whistling and roaring. The warm air met the cold of space and turned into a glittering cloud of sparkling ice crystals. Tom opened his helmet more, breathing dust with the needed air, then reached down and turned on his magnetic boots. He brushed past the hunched crewman and walked out onto the window. In his ear, on the emergency channel, he heard the repairman yell at him, but the young inventor ignored the call.

The strong wind all but toppled him, but he reached the first of the metal struts between the plastic hexes and felt his magnetic shoes take hold. Tom moved along steadily until he could grasp the edge of the inflated patching panel. It was still large enough to cover the hole, although just barely, and it would have to be positioned precisely.

With Tom as an anchor, the others got to their feet and swung the panel over the hole.

The escaping air sought to drag the patch out, but the struggling humans brought it into position. There was an abrupt cessation of wind, and only the loud sucking hiss of the air going under the imperfectly fitted patch broke the silence. The orange-suited repair crew hurried along with big gunlike tubes and foamed out a sealant.

In moments it was done, and Tom heaved a sigh of relief.

"Thanks," one of the repair people said to Tom as they walked off the surface of the window. "That was my first repair job, and I didn't know it was going to be like that."

"You wouldn't have had this job except for me," Tom said unhappily. "I—" Tom was interrupted by a call on the emergency band in his suit radio.

"Tom Swift, report to Doctor Grotz's office at once!"

One of the crewmen pointed toward the far end of the cylinder. "His labs are down there. If you're in a hurry, take an aircycle."

"Aircycle? Oh, one of those?" Tom pointed up. A quarter of a mile over their heads, in the center of the axis of the revolving cylinder, was a tiny figure on a vehicle that looked like a metal insect. The figure pedaled, causing a propeller behind to rotate and push him along.

Rudimentary wings and guide surfaces responded to simple controls.

"There's a hangar up there," continued the crewman. "Just pedal down to the other end. Doctor Grotz's offices are not far below the landing deck."

As Tom walked quickly to the hangar, his face assumed a troubled expression. What would Dr. Grotz do to him? Tom wondered. The accident had been just that—an accident. But the director was known for his sternness, even harshness, to those subordinate to him.

Tom sighed. He certainly did not look forward to facing Dr. Grotz alone, but there was nothing else to do!

Chapter Four

Dr. Hans Grotz was a heavyset man, broad-shouldered and husky, with a slight paunch and hostile eyes. "Look, Swift, I don't care if your father *is* the great Tom Swift," Grotz sneered. Tom felt his anger rising, despite his guilt. "You were careless and stupid, boy."

"Doctor Grotz—"

"Quiet! I am acting director of *New America*. I am responsible for the safety and welfare of its citizens and the security of the entire colony."

"Doctor Grotz, I was testing the smaller version of your own design for the *Daniel Boone*'s drive and—"

"I have always said I am against public access to such information."

38

"But, sir, you had government funding and—"

"Still no reason! *I* created the Prometheus drive, Swift, not some *team*. The way they do research these days is by committee. Each little ant with his or her tiny bite of the pie. Disgusting!" Grotz glared at Tom. "Even you, Swift, can understand that. Your small efforts have been pretty much single-handed. I have to give you that."

"Doctor Grotz, science is so complex that often one person cannot handle the entire—"

"I can!" bellowed Grotz. "I always have, I always will. No little minds are going to drag me down. And you, Swift, you are no longer welcome here. We would appreciate your taking the first shuttle back to Shopton."

"Doctor Grotz," Tom said patiently, "I'm here for the First Annual Space Triangle Race. Since my father—"

"Your father!" interrupted Grotz, snorting.

"Since my father is building the *Daniel Boone*, I thought it might be interesting to test your design. I requested and received permission from your own office here and completed the final fabrication right here in *New America*. You knew I was testing the design and—"

"I did not!" Grotz glared at him. "I can't keep track of every little going-on around here. You shouldn't have been given access."

"Why, Doctor Grotz?" Tom asked quietly. "Your published reports indicated extensive testing and a satisfactory result."

"Yes, and so there was no need for your meddling, Swift."

Tom felt frustration grip him. Talking to Grotz was like talking to a rock. "Doctor, I—"

"That will be all, Swift. Unfortunately, I can't order you to leave." His mouth formed a sour line. "Not without having the great board of directors of Swift Enterprises on my neck. They may not own *New America,* but everyone listens to them. But just one more so-called accident, Swift, and I will send you packing! Be smart, boy—take the next shuttle."

"No, sir, I can't. I've got to find out what went wrong. If it was something I did, some error or miscalculation of mine, I must know. If it was the design, I—"

"The design!" Grotz gripped the edges of his desk and half stood. "There's nothing wrong with the design, Swift! I've been a scientist since before you were born, boy! *You* are going to tell me something is wrong with my design?" Grotz's laugh was harsh, and he sat down again, waving Tom out the door. "Get out. I don't want any more trouble from you, Swift. Stay out of my way, stay out of trouble, and forget any testing or race. Just enjoy the view, then go home."

Tom stood a moment, but Grotz had turned to a large console and was keying up some diagrams. Anger made Tom turn abruptly and stride out of the room, his steps high in the light gravity.

As soon as Grotz heard the door close behind Tom Swift, he sat back in his chair, chuckling to himself. He rather enjoyed being heavy-handed at times. It tended to put fear in the hearts of his enemies, and fear was his most powerful tool for controlling them. Grotz swiveled in his chair and punched the intercom button.

"Wilma, one of the staff authorized the release of the Prometheus drive designs to Tom Swift without informing me. Find out who it was and see that he is given notice, then give that person's responsibilities to Doctor Ellison for reassignment. Don't give any reason. Just make sure that a generous severance check accompanies the pink slip." That should prevent any argument, he thought to himself.

That was the first step. A weak link had been found in his organization, and it must be eliminated. Independent thinkers had no place here. Absolute loyalty was the only acceptable attitude. Take Dr. Greg Ellison, for example. He never disputed any orders; he just followed them. There was a certain amount of hero worship involved, but that made him all the more dependable in the eyes of Hans Grotz.

Grotz frowned. The next thing would have to be the elimination of Tom Swift from the scene. How he hated interference in his plans. And this time, the stakes were especially high—the Nobel Prize! Eventually, he would find and correct the errors in his calculations. He always found and corrected his mistakes before anyone else could discover them. The *Daniel Boone* would launch on time, and he would be the most celebrated scientist in world history—if Tom Swift didn't get in his way. He wouldn't let that happen, no matter what it cost! However, he would leave that to Worden and Deckert. They were experts when it came to "Yankee Go Home" projects.

Outside the administration building, Tom paused, looking out over the tubular length of the colony. *Grotz seemed determined to stop me from checking out his planetary drive,* Tom thought. The young inventor forced himself to be calm. No one likes to be wrongly accused. *But am I wrongly accused? Maybe it was something I did that caused the guidance mechanism to break up.*

Tom sighed and started down the steps toward the traffic control building. He'd find this Ben, whom Tom only knew from several conversations over the ship's radio. Maybe Ben would help plot the angle at which the fragment had hit the window, and Tom could find and study it.

The young Earthman was unused to the light gravity and the steep steps, and was paying more attention to the guard rail and the steps than to who was coming up. He only just stopped short before running into three people. He looked up and was momentarily stunned.

There were two angry young roughnecks and a young woman with thick red hair that framed her face like a brilliant flaming corona.

Her skin was pale and very smooth, and her features had an interesting definition, which caught and held Tom's gaze. She was beautiful, but not in a traditional way. It was a beauty that was heightened and intensified by an obviously high intelligence.

"You're Tom Swift, aren't you?" she said boldly. One of the young men standing next to her sneered at him and took a menacing step forward.

"You're a real celebrity—a celebrity creep!"

Tom looked from the young woman to her two glaring companions and knew this scene would not be pleasant.

"You were testing your racer within the safety zone of the colony. I heard the story on the news," the redhead said harshly. It was obvious to Tom that she was the leader of this group, because the two punks were taking their cues from her.

"I was in an authorized training zone and monitored by Control," Tom replied.

"Yeah, but your fancy little bug blew up," one of the young men snapped.

The redhead stepped closer to Tom. "Listen, Mister Swift, we've heard of you. You're a big honcho down on Earth. But this is *New America*. This is space. There's a different set of rules up here. Dummies who foul things up don't just get themselves killed; they can get a lot of people killed!"

"Look, uh—"

"Thorwald. Anita Thorwald. This race is important to me, but not as important as my life; and I don't like to see someone like you taking chances with it."

"I had an accident," was Tom's only reply. "I'm going to investigate my accident—if it was an accident. Then I'm going to build a new ship . . . and win the race!"

Anita's chin came up. "Oh? How very conceited of you, Swift. I'm in the race, too, and I'm going to win, not you!"

Tom smiled. "That remains to be seen, Ms. Thorwald." He looked at the two young men still glowering at him. "Gentlemen," he said softly. Then he turned and continued down the steps.

"Ben'll be off duty in a few minutes," the secretary said to Tom. "Sorry to hear about your accident," she added.

Tom smiled lopsidedly. "That doesn't seem to be the prevailing opinion. I caused a lot of trouble."

She smiled. "Gives the patch crew some practice. They don't get much practice—thank goodness." She turned back to her console. "Ben'll be coming out that door. Make yourself comfortable."

Tom sat down and considered his problems. He thought he had been very careful in constructing the ship's drive from the plans furnished by Grotz's office. The report he had read seemed to prove this was going to be the great step forward in planetary drives, shortening flights from months to weeks, even days in some cases. Grotz had developed the new concept partially on a grant from the National Science Agency, thereby making his design available for noncommercial use. The early reports on the drive had caused a great deal of excitement. There was talk of a Nobel Prize for Grotz, plus many other awards. Tom thought it was a little early to tell, since the drive had not had a major field test. But if everything did check out, it would be a fantastic achievement.

Where did I go wrong? Tom wondered. I used the newest Langley computer, and everything had been checked out with laser-testing devices to the umpteenth degree of exactitude.

"Hi, you're Tom Swift, right?"

Tom looked up. Before him was a tall, smiling young man, solidly built, with gleaming black hair and light brown skin. His blue jumper was worn, but clean, and there was a tape reader in a small holster at his hip.

"Ben?" Tom asked, getting up.

"Benjamin Franklin Walking Eagle," the young man said, holding out his hand. "Sorry about your accident."

"Look, I could use your help," Tom said. Before the young native American could reply, Tom hurried on. "I have to recover that fragment. Maybe it will tell me what went wrong. Maybe you could backtrack on the orbit and—"

"Whoa." Ben put up a hand and grinned. "I thought of that, and I know where it is. Well, within a few meters, anyway. I was going over there to look. Want to come along?"

"You bet!" Grinning, the two young men left the control dome and walked down toward the factories just below. "Where is it? Was anyone hurt, do you know?"

"Oh, no, everyone's okay. It's in the cornfield,

just beyond the spaceforms warehouse."

They came off the steps and went down a straight factory street. Electric trucks hummed past, carrying loads of raw materials and finished products. The foam-packed electronic equipment was on its way to the main cargo dock, while the trucks were bringing back bars of Moon metal and Earth-made elements for fabrication.

"Benjamin Franklin Walking Eagle," Tom repeated. "What tribe?"

"Cherokee."

"The high-iron people, right?"

Ben grinned. "You know of us, then? Yeah, my ancestors have been climbing around high up for generations. I've had family who worked on the Empire State Building, the Twin Towers of the World Trade Center, and the Sunset Arcolog."

Tom shook his head with a grin. "Funny how one group had this certain special talent."

"Not me, though."

"What do you mean? Isn't that why you're up here?"

"Oh, yeah, sure. My father and I came up early on. Him before me. I was born on Earth, but it seems like I've been up here my whole life. My dad's over on *Sunflower* now."

"And you're in control?"

Ben smiled ruefully. "I can do the high-iron work, it's just that I like other things better."

"Such as?"

"Go right between these two buildings. The farmland starts just beyond. Oh, such as computers. Ever since I can remember, I've been fascinated by them. And they seem to like me." He grinned at Tom.

"There are some people who just have natural ability in certain ways. Like green thumbs or luck with cards or playing music, or art," Tom said. "Yours is in computers, huh?"

Ben answered eagerly, pleased with Tom's interest. "I . . . well, it sounds conceited to say it, but . . . well, I *am* good. I can write programs in a flash. I'm awfully good at getting facts out of a computer—"

He stopped at Tom's frown. "You think all you have to do is ask a computer something and it answers right off, huh? A lot of people believe that . . . including, I'm afraid, other computer people. No, you see, a computer is dumb. It's very fast, it never forgets, but that's *all* it can do, despite all the new stuff about computers having independent thought. So far they don't have creative thought. They simply put together old thoughts, old facts, in new ways."

"Isn't that what humans do, too?"

"Yes, sometimes, but the human mind is incredibly complex and far more creative than any computer. What I can do, though, is ask a computer the right question."

"The right question?"

"Uh-huh. See, computers can't hide things. Not even computers with secret instructions. Given time, you can get around the most complex security system. Given time." Ben grinned at Tom.

They came to a halt at the edge of a huge cornfield. "This is an experimental field. They're forcing growth, getting more yield per acre. We use everything, of course, not just the cobs. Stalks, roots, tassel, everything. It's all cellulose and sugar, after all." He pointed. "I think the fragment should be over there."

As they slipped carefully through the closely planted crop, Tom found the first evidence. "Look, broken stalks!"

The piece of wrecked metal was buried under a foot of soft soil, with the broken green stalks pointing right to it. Tom scraped the soil away and looked at the lump of partially melted metal. "It's a piece of the chamber housing." Turning it over in his hands, he brushed off bits of compacted earth. The ground smelled good, moist and fragrant, and a breeze stirred the stalks noisily. Without any wind at all, Tom knew, the stalks would grow weakly and be unable to support themselves well, much less the heavy corncobs.

"Do you think I could use the lab here?" Tom asked.

"Oh, sure! I have a friend working there. He'd

be glad to let Tom Swift work—if he could watch."

Tom was embarrassed by the admiration evident in Ben's words and manner. "Uh ... great," he said, hefting the shard of broken drive.

"Come on, I'll take you there."

Tom stood up and brushed the soil from his trousers. He followed Ben back through the waving stalks, fingering the piece of metal. Would he be able to find out what he needed to know from it? Could this scrap of his ship provide the vital secret? It had to, it just *had* to. There was no other way he could get the information, information he desperately needed!

Chapter Five

Tom sat on the lab bench and stared gloomily at the only piece of his ship left. With a laser he had sliced off a section for analysis and subjected it to several tests. Then he had cut another bit for stress tests, chemical immersion, and X-rays. It didn't tell him much, only that there had been an explosion, but not really why.

Tom Swift felt very alone.

His father was unavailable. Ben's friend, Chang Yen, was noticeably cold toward Tom, acting as if he had been betrayed in some way. Grotz was spreading the word that Tom was a troublemaker and a danger to the colony.

And now a dead end in the analysis. He still didn't know why the drive had exploded. Quickly, he reviewed the general possibilities. Design failure: undecided, insufficient information. Overload: he had not been near the danger point, though he had been pushing toward a stress point. Material flaw: he had used the best available materials, atomically pure metal, high-stress plastic, and so on. It was unlikely, but not impossible.

Tom scratched his cheek. As unpleasant as it was there were really only two other possibilities: pilot error and ... sabotage. But he hadn't been doing anything particularly risky, he had proceeded normally—monitored and careful.

That left sabotage.

But who? And why? The obvious suspects were others in the race, but that didn't seem likely either. None of the young pilots he had met seemed the kind to endanger, much less kill, anyone.

Tom slapped his hand down on the lab bench and grunted. Nothing! *Insufficient information,* as a computer would say. Tom got up and walked thoughtfully out of the small lab, nodding to Ben's friend and saying he was finished.

"Thanks," Tom added.

The young technician nodded, not looking up. Tom went on out. He stopped on the balcony and looked at *New America* all around him. This giant tin can in the sky was suspended in a real frontier—space. It was a frontier that Daniel

Boone would never have recognized and it was limitless. Worlds beyond worlds.

The space ship *Daniel Boone* would be the first manned exploration out beyond dry, cold Mars. It was not to be one or two astronauts in a cramped capsule. The trip was too long for that, and too expensive. The *Daniel Boone* was big enough to carry a crew and a complement of scientists. They would explore and test, dig and observe, take samples and pictures, and open up a dozen or more moons to exploration. Probes had been sent into the interior of that great, wondrously colorful world of Jupiter, and equipment pods were now on their way to her moons in anticipation of the maiden voyage of the *Daniel Boone.* Months would be spent there, farther out than man had ever gone from his home. Expensive months, but vastly rewarding ones.

The young scientist began walking down toward the temporary quarters, a brisk mile walk along the central city. The night cycle was approaching, and shifts of people were coming off work, laughing and talking. Some looked curiously at Tom. Only a few smiled. There was some muttering, but Tom didn't catch many words. He kept his gaze on the sidewalk and put his hands in his pockets.

A blare of music made him look up. A brightly colored dome was pulsating with light in time to the pounding rhythm. Gaily dressed young people were going in. Tom hesitated, then walked on. A hologram theater was playing a remake of a great old cavalry film, *She Wore a Yellow Ribbon,* along with a documentary, *Riding the Colorado River.* The holographic images were quite realistic, almost like being there, and the nature tapes were very popular in all the space stations and colonies.

Tom walked on, isolated and insulated against the gaiety of those around him. It took him a moment to realize someone was talking to him.

"I said, hello there, young fella."

It was the old man who had been at the emergency entrance when Tom had come in after the accident.

"Oh, hi," Tom said.

"You did well on that patch job," the man said. "I watched ya. Good thinking, young fella."

"Uh, thank you. But it was my fault to begin with."

"Uh-huh." The man fell in step next to Tom. He aimed a thumb back at the lighted part of the small city. "All the action is back there, young fella."

"Yes, I know. But, I ... I don't feel much like it."

"Know what you mean. My name's Phil Castora."

"Tom Swift." They shook hands.

"I know your dad. Knew him, anyway. Years ago. He got me the job when this whole thing was in the construction-shack phase. Saved my life."

Tom raised his eyebrows inquiringly. Castora tapped his chest. "Bad ticker. Up here, the gravity's less; less strain on the heart. If things get bad, I just go up to the ends and float around a bit. Wonderful invention, null-gravity. Got to watch your diet, though. You can get fat as a pig, not really having to carry any of your weight around."

Tom nodded, distracted, still thinking about what had gone wrong with his ship.

"That construction-shack time, that was something." Castora stamped his foot on the ground. "Didn't have this then. No protection from solar flares, unless you got to a shelter in time. Sometimes people didn't make it. You hardly had any warning at all. One of the first things we set up was the solar observatory. It was pure self-protection, no real research done, just a steady twenty-four-hour watch. Slap the emergency signal, and we'd drop whatever we were doing and dive for cover." He waved his hand around. "Not like now. You might not even know there'd been one unless you saw it on the evening news."

Tom nodded again. "Well, Tom, I'll see you around, I guess." The man turned off, giving a wave, and Tom felt still guiltier. Had he offended him? He hadn't meant to, but he was so caught up in the accident that—

"Get that Swift creep!"

They came out of a side street, three of them, masked and armed with what looked like lengths of aluminum bar stock—solid aluminum pipe used to make machined shafts in a lathe. Tom didn't have much time to think. They came right at him, brandishing the bright weapons, swinging at his head.

Instead of backing up, Tom drove forward, surprising them. He threw a wide blocking smash into the legs of two of them, and everyone fell in a yelling jumble. Tom felt a blow across his leg, then blocked a swing from the one man left standing. Someone punched him in the side, then he was pulling free and rolling away. He got to his feet and attacked at once, jumping high and kicking out, smashing his foot into the chest of the nearest attacker. The man gasped and lay quiet. Tom landed on his feet, whirled and just missed kicking the second attacker.

A bar of metal whizzed by his head, and Tom turned to meet the third assailant. The man waggled the bar at him, feinted, then swung again, but Tom danced back. The second man drove in at him, swinging the metal club viciously. Tom could not avoid all the impact of the blow, but diverted most of the force with his forearm, striking up against the other's fist. The bar tumbled from his fingers with a clatter.

The third man came in fast, forcing Tom back and away from the dropped weapon. Tom ducked and weaved, aware that he was being pressed back against the garden wall of a nearby home. He heard a shout from the house. "Hey, what's this? What are you guys doing?"

Tom jumped forward and struck out with the edge of his hand at the wrist of the man before him. The metal bar fell with a clang and the man turned to run. The second attacker hurled his recovered bar of metal at Tom, who ducked, but felt the pain of a blow across his shoulder. In seconds, all three were gone, melted into the side street, into the artificial night.

"What's going on?" A man came out of the house behind Tom, a flashlight in his hand.

"I don't know," Tom said, rubbing at his shoulder and taking the weight off his hurt leg.

"Hooligans? Thieves? I don't believe it," the man said. "That's one of the reasons I came up here, to get away from things like that! They hurt you, son?"

"No, I'm all right." Tom bent over and picked up one of the bars of aluminum. "Where would anyone get things like these?"

The man beamed his flashlight on the metal. "Oh, most anywhere. Moon metal, you know. People don't lock things up much up here." He peered closely at Tom's face, shining the light on him. "You're a visitor, aren't you? Oh, right, you're that Swift boy. Saw you on the news tonight. Too bad about that break. Tough luck." He gestured toward the vanished attackers. "Never knew people would get that worked up about it!"

"Neither did I." Tom thanked the man and walked on, holding the aluminum bar thoughtfully. Was that the reason? Was someone angry at Tom's endangering the colony? Or was there another reason?

Chapter Six

The wallscreen buzzed.

Tom put down the videotape reader, showing a page from *Stress Analysis Factors in Metallic Substances Formed in Gravitationless Environments.* He picked up the remote control. The big screen blinked into life, revealing an enormous head shot of Benjamin Franklin Walking Eagle.

"Hi, Ben," Tom said listlessly.

The dark-haired young man laughed. "You sound very up and excited."

Tom smiled warily and nodded.

"I think you've been cooped up there too long, being a scientific detective and all that."

"I've got to figure out what went wrong," Tom replied.

"Gremlins," Ben said with authority. "They

migrated into space just about the same time we did." His smile faded. "Look, you must get out, at least a little. Ever play null-gravity handball?"

"No." Suddenly the idea of a little physical activity seemed inviting. Although he was not a fanatic, Tom liked to play sports. "Is this an invitation?"

"It is. Meet me at the aircycle landing at the south end in twenty minutes."

"Okay!" Ben waved and the screen flicked back to its usual neutral, beige color. Tom crossed the tiny living room of his guest quarters, removing his clothes as he went. He stepped into the electronic shower and flicked the switch. Sixteen small cones bathed his athletic body in invisible, unheard waves. All foreign particles were given a negative electrical charge and jumped immediately to the collector strips which flanked him on the shower's walls. At once he felt refreshed and clean.

It's no substitute for a nice hot shower, Tom thought, but it certainly saves a lot of energy and water. He turned off the machine and stepped out of the booth to dress in a clean white jumper. He pulled on some worn, comfortable sneakers and quickly left his quarters.

The barrackslike building was only a short walk from the tram that regularly circled the inside of the colony. He jumped aboard and held on to a support as the machine hummed along the highway that ran from one end of the colony to the other.

Tom jumped off the tram at the south-end stop and trotted up the steps quickly, losing gravity with each step. It was a feeling of exhilaration that he had not grown used to. When his feet no longer were making any real contact, he began to pull himself along in long, gliding runs, using the poles by the steps.

He paused partway up for breath and to have another look at *New America*. It wasn't Earth, and it was touching that they so obviously had tried to imitate it. Rugged hills at each end, rivers and lakes, parks and highways—a synthetic Terra, manicured and carefully designed. There were no snakes to cast out of this paradise— none had been let in. Nor had any annoying or harmful insects. Bees, yes, to pollinate the trees and flowers. Earthworms and bacteria that made the sterile Moon soil live. Birds and their seriocomic foe, cats. Lots of cats, but only a dog or two. A few pet turtles, Tom had heard, some snails, and one spider monkey. And cockroaches.

Tom grimaced. He supposed that even when mankind got to the stars themselves, cockroaches would somehow manage to tag along.

Tom started up the steep steps again, pulling himself along in what was now a practiced routine. He came out on the aircycle deck and at once saw Ben Walking Eagle standing and talking to two other people.

But as Tom came closer he realized that Ben was arguing with the volatile redhead, Anita Thorwald, and someone Tom did not recognize. They stopped when they saw him approach in long, slow leaps. Tom overestimated his velocity, and Ben had to grab him just before he crashed into a rack of aircycles.

"Oof!"

Ben laughed, and Tom apologized. "Sorry. This swimming around in no gravity is something I'm not used to."

Anita Thorwald sniffed, holding delicately on to a stanchion. "So you just barge in as always, blundering through everything, eh, Swift?"

Tom held his temper and ignored her. "I'm Tom Swift," he said to Anita's companion.

"Mark Scott," the young man said. He was barrel-chested, slightly plump, and had a full mustache, and his smile was friendly.

"I think you know Anita Thorwald," Ben said with a sly smile. "One of our more vocal advocates of Space for the Spacers."

The redhead gave Ben a withering look, but the Indian computerman was already taking Tom toward a pole that led up from the aircycle deck to a large geodesic globe at the exact center of the longitudinal axis, where the gravity would be at the absolute minimum.

"I've booked us for an hour," Ben said, "but we'll have to wait a few minutes. Give you a chance to see how it's done."

"Oh, you mean Swift won't just charge in and start playing competition handball right off?" muttered Anita.

Ben took Tom to a window on a catwalk around the globe. The catwalks were all light-weight tubes of metallic grid, and a maze of them crisscrossed the entire outside surface of the globe. Triangular windows were set into the pattern made by the interlocking sections of the struts.

Inside Tom could see a four-person team working hard. The entire inner surface of the globe was smooth, broken only by the triangular windows. Areas were painted off in green, blue, yellow, and black. A thick red line bisected the globe into two hemispheres, and it was back and forth across this line the jumper-clad figures leaped and plunged.

The gymnastics were spectacular; the players performed convoluted actions undreamed of by even the best professionals bound by Terran gravity. Ben pointed. "The black areas are off limits and there is an electronic sensor mat under each, so that there is no question of calling the shot. The yellow areas are two points off. Green and blue are okay for you or not, depending on which team you are on. One point off for touching the opponent's color. The ball must rebound off the hemisphere opposite from which it began before you can hit it."

"There's a sensor in the ball?" Tom asked.

Ben nodded. "The ball can touch any color but the black, and there's a hairline sensor in the center of the red line, just so there's no need for judgment calls." He grinned at Tom. "Not quite like squash or handball down below, is it?"

Tom said, "Not quite," and smiled. "By the way, what were you and the redhead fighting about?"

"You," Ben said casually. "I think your head on a pike is what she had in mind. She cannot be counted among your more ardent admirers."

"*I'm* not even among my ardent admirers," Tom replied. "Not these days."

"Aw, Tom, why don't you—"

"Hey, guys," Mark called out. The team inside had finished, and the last member was rebounding from the wall to float gracefully toward the triangular hatch which had opened.

"Come on. This will be fun," Ben said.

They launched themselves into the sphere. Tom saw each of his companions do a flip in midair, land on his feet against the opposite surface, and then rebound into the center with carefully controlled exertion. They floated, waiting for Tom.

He shoved off and tried to do his flip just as they had, but he pushed off too hard and the opposite wall came up faster than he had anticipated. He hit hard, rekindling the pain in his thigh where the thugs had struck him, and bounced awkwardly out into the room. Anita laughed and made no attempt to hide her amusement.

"Close hatch," Ben said, and the automatic devices obeyed. "Ready, Tom?" Ben asked. "You and I are Alpha, Anita and Mark are Omega. Don't touch the blue. Ready?"

"As ready as I'll ever be," Tom said, and Anita snickered loudly.

"Start ball," Ben said.

A small, circular hatch slid open, right on the red line, and a black ball was spat out. A random-number tape sent the ball to one side of the red line or the other.

"Ours," Mark said. The ball bounced back, and Anita did a somersault in midair, coming out of it to strike the ball perfectly and send it sailing across the sphere. The equal and opposite reaction of her movement and blow sent her back, and she did a backflip and touched down on the inner surface, carefully straddling the point of a black triangle. She came gracefully back out, turning vertically as she did.

The ball came at Tom quickly, but he was used to the speed of handball from the hours he had spent in rectangular courts back on Earth. What he wasn't used to was not having gravity to push against, as it were. He swung at the ball and moved helplessly away, waving his arm wildly to recover his balance, but succeeding only in disorienting himself and tumbling. He bounced off a green triangle and lunged helplessly to the side, brushing a blue triangle with his shoulder. He heard a tiny, bell-like sound and saw the grin on Anita's face.

Embarrassed and frustrated, Tom righted himself and shoved off the surface just as the black ball came whizzing at him from Mark's hefty blow. He batted at it, sending it back with a sizzle, but as he floated backward from the force of the blow, he heard Ben groan. "It hadn't rebounded off the other hemisphere, Tom."

"Strike while the ball is hot, eh, Swift?" Anita jeered.

Tom floundered around for several more moments, thudding into the wall and stepping on another blue triangle. They were six points behind when Ben made the first score. Then Tom surprised everyone—including himself—by very expertly firing the ball between Mark and Anita to bounce into an area they could not reach in time.

But that was his last score. The first game ended twelve to four, and the second game was no better. They took a break, and Ben called out for refreshments. A smoothly fitted hatch opened, and a dispenser offered small plastic globes of chilled water with sipping straws built in. Water in a glass, Tom knew, would probably climb out of it and bobble around in a great sphere, held together by surface tension; the only way to drink was to sip through a straw.

"They're killing us," Ben said, in a good-natured way.

"All my fault," Tom said. He shook his head wearily. *Everything* was going wrong.

"Are you kidding?" Ben said. "You should have seen me when I started! I flapped like a duck and almost dislocated my shoulder trying not to hit the black. Listen, you're ahead of where I was after a score of games. It's something you have a knack for, obviously. You play a dozen or so games, and I bet you'll be giving pointers to the best around here."

"Don't try to make me feel better, Ben. I'm about as graceful as a cement block. Did you see the way Anita did that recovery? Pure ballet. This must be the most graceful, as well as the fastest, game in the entire solar system."

"Uh-huh," agreed Ben. "But don't knock yourself. You've gotten better since the first game. Think you could even have tried that back-flip when you came in here?"

Tom shook his head. "It doesn't feel like I'm getting better. Anita and Mark are making a fool out of me. You better get another partner."

"No way, Tom. We'll book some time tomorrow and just practice. I'll show you how to control your rebound so that you're in just the area you want to be, okay?" He grinned. "Listen, give you a hundred games like me, and you'll be going out for the Olympics."

Tom looked at his new friend. "I didn't know null-gravity handball was in the Olympics."

"It isn't, but it ought to be, and it will someday. I've got a friend over in Telecommunications who's trying to get our colony playoffs on the World Network next time. Once people watch us, it'll get popular."

"Only in space, Ben. It's one game that will be a spectator sport to ninety-nine percent of the people."

"So's hockey or chess or boxing. You wait and see. Well, ready to try again?"

Tom shrugged and floated away from the dispenser, then grabbed for it. "Sure. Why not? There's nothing I like better than smashing into a wall with my face."

Tom and Ben only lost the third game by four points and the fourth game by three. Maybe everything isn't going bad, Tom thought as they went out through the exit hatch. Maybe I've rebounded and am starting back up, he hoped.

Chapter Seven

Tom and Ben sat silently across from each other at Ben's desk, both thinking hard and getting nowhere. They were convinced that there was a fatal flaw somewhere in Grotz's drive design. The trouble was, they didn't know where.

"Let's stop thinking about this for a while," Ben said, heaving himself up. "I've been looking at these wiring diagrams and the printouts from your lost ship for so long that I can hardly see."

"You're right," admitted Tom. He switched off the big television screen holding the diagrams. "If we keep pushing ourselves like this, we're going to miss something important."

"Tom, have you tried to contact your father again?" Ben asked.

Tom's expression became serious. "No. I've temporarily given up on that."

"I think you're wrong not to contact him. If the *Daniel Boone* is going to explode in a great ball of flame minutes out of port, your father ought to know about it. Anyway, Tom, I'm starved! Let's go out to eat tonight and get away from here for a while. On our way back, we can stop at Telecommunications and place a call to Earth."

"Well . . ."

"Tom, you look so down on your luck, and it's not going to help your situation at all to stay in this frame of mind. You're defeated before you even start."

"Right, coach!"

"Seriously, I think your problem is that you've been spending too much time alone in the temporary quarters. That place is so sterile, environment-wise, that it would depress anybody. Besides, staying up there, you're out of touch with what's really happening in *New America*. I want you to move in with me!"

"But . . ."

"No 'buts.' I haven't had a roomie for a long time, and I sort of miss it. There's plenty of room here, and I think it will do you some good. We'll pick up your stuff after we visit Telecom."

"Ben, listen to me," Tom said. He watched

Ben turn out the lights in his quarters, and he felt himself sinking deeper into the pit of depression. He was beginning to feel like a burden to his new friend, and he didn't like the feeling at all. "I appreciate your offer, but I might as well have the Black Death when it comes to social interaction around here! Doctor Grotz has done a pretty thorough job of making me an official 'untouchable.' I don't want any of my social soot rubbing off on you."

"Hey, let me worry about that, okay?"

"I don't know . . ."

"It's settled then," Ben said, looking at Tom firmly. "Listen, let's go eat! I know a great Italian restaurant that's not too far from here—the *Via Nuova America.* Do you like spaghetti?"

"Ben," Tom said, exasperated. But Benjamin Franklin Walking Eagle was already out the front door.

Two hours later, Tom and Ben were entering the telecommunications center.

"Excuse my garlic breath," Tom laughed. Ben chuckled and made a show of moving away from Tom.

"I warned you that the *fettuccine verdi con pesto* was potent. I'll thank you to keep at least five paces away from me for the rest of the night!"

The two young men were still laughing as they approached the main information desk, where a pretty, brunette receptionist sat smiling at them.

"I'd like to call person-to-person to Swift Enterprises, on Earth," Tom told her. He fished in his wallet for a few seconds and then presented his *New America* identification card to her.

The receptionist placed the card in the top of a machine that had a small viewscreen and waited. A few seconds later, a light blinked, and the receptionist took the card out and placed it in a slot marked BOOTH FIVE.

"I'll keep your card until you're finished, Mister Swift. Take booth five and ... wait." she added as Ben and Tom turned to go. "Take these too. Take the whole package," she said, smiling broadly as she held out a half-used roll of breath mints. Tom took them, blushing furiously.

Communications inside *New America* were not complicated. Local calls could be made from any telephone in the colony. Calling outside the colony was another matter. If the target was on the far side of Earth from the colony, the signal had to be bounced to a couple of satellites, strengthened, then beamed by tight microwave to Earth.

Booth five contained a large console and a viewscreen, below which were a focusing microphone and a camera pickup lens. Tom punched a button for the directory, then one for the North American directory. A few more fingertip maneuvers gave Tom the routing for the call. Then he punched the code for the Swift Enterprises main office and his father's office in particular. A few moments later, the private secretary smiled at Tom.

"Hello, Tom! How are you doing up there?"

"Fine. May I speak to my father?"

Her face sobered. "Unless this is an extreme emergency, I'm really unable to reach your father. We made him get some sleep before he collapsed from exhaustion. There was some kind of undersea landslide. It cut the cable, and all the regular channels were too busy with emergency traffic to get through before. Is there anyone else who can help you? I can have your father return the call when he wakes up."

Tom looked distressed. "Yes, please, have him call me, if he can. No, it's not an emergency. Well, so long, and . . . wait!" Tom sat up quickly. "Yes, there is someone. Put me through to Gene Larson."

The secretary's eyebrows went up in surprise. "Tom, he's pretty busy out in the field right now . . ."

"Marguerite, I've got to talk to someone!"

The secretary sighed, and nodded. The screen flicked to the Swift Enterprises hold pattern.

"Gene Larson," Ben said softly as they waited. "That's a name to strike terror into the hearts of any up-and-coming scientists."

"He's my father's chief troubleshooter and about the most straightforward guy I know," Tom said. "When you ask him to investigate something, he doesn't pull any punches." Tom shrugged. "That's how he got his reputation for being, well, hard-nosed. People sometimes think he's—"

Tom stopped as the screen flicked from the hold pattern to blue sky, against which they could see the tilted rectangles of a rectenna farm somewhere on the surface of Earth. Someone in a loose-fitting, crinkly foil protection suit was speaking to someone else out of camera and microphone range. Then the figure turned, and Tom recognized Gene Larson beneath the hood that gave added protection when one was in a target area for microwave transmissions from the solar-power satellites. The suits, somewhat like raincoats with hoods, gave workers extended time under the beams from space.

Larson's piercing blue eyes seemed to look straight into Tom's. "What is it now, Tom?" the big man said brusquely.

"Uh . . ." Tom had steeled himself for the characteristic abruptness of this man he had known all his life, but he was totally unprepared for the cold, biting edge in the man's voice. It shook him up. "Um, Gene, I'm sorry to bother you, but I've had some problems up here that I think you should know about."

"If you're talking about your personality conflict with Doctor Grotz, I don't want to—"

"Personality conflict?" Tom blurted out the words, interrupting the older man. "Where did you hear that?"

Larson's face was impassive. "Doctor Grotz beamed a pretty thorough report down to us about this whole mess you've gotten yourself into. He thinks you're acting like an irresponsible rich kid. He's requested that we call you home."

The anger boiled up in Tom. It was so unfair. "And what do you think?" Tom asked, barely able to restrain himself from yelling. He was righteously angry that Dr. Grotz had seen fit to carry his case to Tom's home, as if Tom were a child. He was young, yes, but it had been some time since he had needed a baby-sitter. Tom had not sensed the depth of Grotz's inexplicable hatred until now.

"I have no opinion," Larson said evenly. "I don't know all the facts. Is this what you called to talk about?"

Tom took a deep breath to steady his voice and his nerves. Gene Larson had always been the man, second only to Tom's father, that Tom had sought to please and gain approval from. He felt betrayed. "No, Gene," he said levelly. "It's more serious. A friend of mine and I—"

"Ben Walking Eagle?"

"Yes. We've done some preliminary investigation, and we think there's something dangerously wrong with Doctor Grotz's space drive."

"What is it?" Larson demanded.

"We don't know exactly . . ."

There was a flicker of annoyance on Larson's stern face. "That's a stiff charge to make about someone with Grotz's reputation and credentials when you can't back up your accusation with solid proof. It's not like you to have your case this badly prepared."

The words stung Tom, but he plunged on. "I know, but we've got to stop the drive installation on the *Daniel Boone* right away—or a lot of people will be killed . . . including my father."

"You're coming at this from an emotional base, Tom," Larson said. "That's always a weak position to argue from."

"This isn't a high school debate, Gene."

"You're sure right it isn't!" Larson said, raising his voice for the first time, startling Tom. "I'm trying to get you to use your head, boy! You dislike Doctor Grotz because he's giving you a hard time, and you're letting it interfere with your work instead of proceeding in a scientific manner!"

Larson's voice softened a touch. "Look, Tom, you've come through with some pretty remarkable things in the past, and you know that when you say there's something wrong, we're going to sit up and take a look down here. And it isn't just because you're the boss's son. But we have to have more than just your word, your suspicion."

Larson's tone was friendly, but still there was the touch of authority in it. "I know you put a lot of time into developing that fusion drive of yours, then Grotz came along and took the wind out of your sails. His invention just seemed to leapfrog ahead, right past conventional development. I can understand your being annoyed, but—"

"That's not the reason, Gene! There really is something wrong. Not, I admit, according to all his published papers on it, or according to his tests. But my ship shouldn't have blown up. And why is Grotz so antagonistic? And why—"

"Tom," Larson said harshly, stopping him. "Tom, get proof. Give us numbers, data, test results, something. You understand?"

Tom sat back in his chair and stared at the screen in silence for a few seconds. When he spoke his voice was calm. "Thanks for your time, Gene. Sorry to bother you. Please tell my father

I called." Larson nodded, and Tom ended the transmission.

Ben whistled softly.

"He's right, Ben," Tom said quietly. "He's absolutely correct. You were trying to tell me the same thing back at your quarters, but it didn't sink in until just now."

Tom felt his jaw thoughtfully. "This is war. Doctor Grotz declared it, and I've been in retreat the whole time. There are too many lives at stake for me to go on doing that. I've got to start fighting like a professional—or lose!"

Tom stood up and grinned at his new friend. "Let's pick up my stuff from the temporary quarters now. We can make the move in one trip."

Ben smiled and then walked out, thanking the telecommunications operator.

"What's this about a fusion drive you developed?" Ben asked as they walked along.

"Something I had almost finished. I was about to start testing, but then Grotz's drive came out and it seemed to be so much more efficient. Well . . ." Tom shrugged.

They were silent a moment, then Tom said, "Let's talk about the race. I'm going to need a new racer."

"And a whole new drive."

"The racer itself won't be much trouble. After all, it's not much more than an air bubble with a big push behind it."

Ben rolled his eyes. "Oh, if Wernher von Braun could have heard you. How casually we are taking the wonders of science."

"A century ago they thought that the internal-combustion engine was the greatest, and there were shade-tree mechanics everywhere ... but that same car a century earlier would have seemed wondrous indeed."

"So much for the history of science." Ben smiled. "And what are you going to use for a drive, your own invention?"

"I've been thinking—"

"When aren't you thinking, Tom Swift?"

"It's hard to stop thinking, Ben. It's one thing I have never mastered. Look, the conventional rocket engine is a very large and wasteful device; the chemical rocket is very old-fashioned. So's the ion drive."

"The ion drive is old-fashioned?" exclaimed Ben.

"Yup. Are you familiar with how the ion engine works?" When Ben shrugged, Tom grabbed a pad and started drawing quick, sure diagrams. "Look, you charge an electron negatively, then propel it along a track magnetically. You do that a lot of times, very fast, and you move in the opposite direction. There's a little more to it than that—such as emitting some electrons to combat the particles coming back, but that's it, basically."

"How fast is fast?"

"A few thousand times a second. At least. The more the better, and the faster you go. But I think I have something better. I've been working on it. We start with Mighty Mouse—that's what I call my fusion drive . . ."

"A fusion drive?"

"Uh-huh. Oh, I know, others have been working on it. The principle is nothing new, but I think I've solved the big problem—guidance and control. I pretty much stopped research and development when Doctor Grotz's drive research was published." Tom's face became very solemn. "I think that's what went wrong, why my ship exploded. The plasma stream just was not properly controlled. But we'll go into that—"

"We?"

"We. You and I. I'll need the tightest patch possible to the best computer we can get. The tolerances on this are pretty slim. Only a computer can give us what we need . . . and a computer is only as good as the person who jockeys it."

"Me?"

"You."

Ben blushed and grinned. "Okay, I'm your man. Where do we get this Mighty Mouse?"

"There's one here now. I ordered it up right after my racer blew up. I've even got a name for it."

Ben smiled. "Everything gets a tag these days. People personify their computers, their aircycles, their . . . Oh well, what's it called?"

"Well, since we both hope to go out on the *Daniel Boone,* and a ship such as we hope to build will be a great scout ship, I thought to call it the *Davy Cricket.*"

"The *Davy Cricket,*" Ben repeated slowly, shaking his head. "Not the *Santa Maria* or the *Beagle* or the *Argos,* not the *Enterprise.* The *Davy Cricket?*"

"You don't like it?"

"Well, most of the racers are called the *Martian Flash* or the *Emmy-Sue* or the *Moonglow* or something."

"So what's wrong with the *Davy Cricket?*"

Ben shrugged. "Nothing, I guess." He shook his head. "*Davy Cricket.*"

"You have to understand that people have had fusion plants for some time," Tom went on to say. "It's just that no one's been able to make one into a successful spaceship drive. The Prometheus drive is a fusion drive, although Grotz and I approached the problem of the magnetic bottle differently."

"What is a magnetic bottle?"

"In theory, it's simple, Ben. You freeze heavy hydrogen—deuterium—into a pellet. You fire this pellet into a spherical magnetic field. The two things are 'blind' to each other, by the way, in the sense that they do not act on or react to each other."

"You can use 'heavy water' too, can't you? That's water in which the hydrogen atoms have been replaced by deuterium."

Tom nodded. "It's easy to handle and potent. You compress the spherical magnetic field, and this causes heat, a *lot* of heat. Comparable to the center of a sun, in fact. There's a thermonuclear reaction. You open up one end of the magnetic bottle, and out comes a flame hot enough to strip molecules to atoms."

"A rocket," Ben said.

"A simplified explanation, yes. The problem has always been two-fold: controlling the magnetic bottle so that there is a completely even push in every direction, and opening up the bottle to let out the plasma stream. They can do it in mining operations, but it takes massive machinery and they don't need the refined control a spaceship requires."

"You solved that?"

"I think so. I'll soon know." They stopped to let an electrocart move by, laden with crates of foam-steel plates. Tom frowned suddenly, and Ben followed his gaze. "That fellow over there . . ."

"Chet Worden?"

"Yes. I met him with Anita Thorwald, but . . .

there's something familiar about him." As they watched, a second young man came out of a protein-processing plant, running his hands through his dark, curly hair. He joined Chet Worden.

"That other one is Dan Deckert," Ben said. "They've built a racer, too. The *Régine*, I think." He looked at Tom. "Something wrong?"

"I've seen them before, I think, and not just with Anita." Suspicions crowded in. Were they the masked men who had attacked him? They were familiar—the way they moved, their size and shape, their body language.

Tom saw Worden and Deckert watching them as they walked away. A scowl crossed Worden's face and he said something to Deckert who nodded in response, his eyes never leaving Tom. Were they his attackers? Tom wondered.

Chapter Eight

The next morning, Tom was breakfasting alone at the neighborhood cafeteria.

He took a sip of his hot drink and thought about his situation as he ate. His first night in Ben's quarters had been the most restful since the accident. He was glad to be mentally back on the ball. But now he had to organize his plan of attack. How would he prove that Dr. Grotz's drive would fail? Could he perfect his own fusion drive in time?

The cafeteria was crowded with the rush from the morning work shift. People in color-coded uniforms sat in clusters, along with others in more casual clothing. He noticed that all the tables were crowded—except his. No one had asked him to join them when he came in, and 85 no one had joined him. In a way he was glad, because he really wanted to do some thinking. So he concentrated and routinely started to block out the surrounding noise, a trick he was glad he had mastered.

"May I sit here?"

Tom looked up from his plate and almost choked on a bite of English muffin. Anita Thorwald stood before him, holding her breakfast tray.

"I said—"

"I heard you. Please, uh, Ms. Thorwald, won't you join me?"

Anita sat down opposite Tom and began eating without looking up. Tom watched her in silence for a few moments, then he spoke. "I don't understand what you have against me, Ms. Thorwald."

The pretty redhead looked up suddenly, as though surprised that Tom was still there, and blinked in annoyance. "I don't like people who make costly mistakes, Mister Swift."

"Call me Tom."

"I know you think that just because you're good-looking and rich, I'll forget what happened and let you win me over with charm!" She leaned forward, slightly frowning. "Well, *Mister* Swift, it won't work! Maybe you can call up Daddy and order up a new toy every time you break one, but that doesn't make me respect you!"

Tom had never been sensitive about being wealthy, because he had contributed significantly to that wealth from his own efforts many times. But Anita's open hostility stung him. She must have sensed an advantage, because she smiled triumphantly and returned purposefully to her meal.

Tom tried again. "Anyone can make a mistake. I helped repair the damage I did, and I'm having the repair costs billed to me. And I didn't have to call 'Daddy' to bail me out. I clean up my own messes!"

"So you do," was Anita's only reply, delivered in a monotone.

Tom paused, looking at her. "You know, we've gotten off to a bad start, and I'm sorry for that."

Anita glanced up at Tom and her large hazel eyes seemed to probe into him for a moment.

"You know a lot about me, but I don't know anything about you. What do you do here? Where are you from?" Tom asked.

Instead of answering, Anita patted her mouth with a napkin and stood up. She picked up her tray and looked down at him. "I've got to go to work now, Mister Swift. It's been nice talking to you."

"Wait!" Tom jumped up so fast he sloshed his orange juice onto the table. Heads turned to stare, some curious, some hostile. They all quickly turned away.

"May I walk with you?" Tom asked, catching up with her.

"It's a free colony," she replied.

Tom dumped his refuse in the bin and stacked his tray above hers. They walked in silence until they reached the biomechanical sciences building.

Tom followed Anita in, somewhat to her surprise, but she said nothing. She greeted some others with a wave and sat down at a well-lighted workbench. Her fellow workers examined Tom and then returned to work.

On the table were components Tom did not recognize. They seemed to be electronic mostly, but they were also fused with linked mechanical parts. Tom looked around as Anita swung a ring-lighted magnifier into place. The lab was large, filled with benches and parts bins. A quiet melody was being broadcast.

Finally Tom said, "All right, you got me. What do you do here?"

"We're an experimental division. Grants from the World Heart Association, the American Medical Association, Stanford, the Asimōv School of Space Medicine . . ." She waved a free hand, still intent on the device under her magnifier.

Tom knew the ice between them had been somewhat chipped away. "Yes, but what do you do?"

Anita swung a tiny television camera into position and snapped it on, then punched up the image on a screen mounted over the workbench. "We build prosthetics, Mister Swift."

"There must be more to it than that—and will you please stop calling me 'Mister Swift'?"

Anita made a vague gesture with a hand tool, and Tom thought she might be blushing. No, that couldn't be.

"I'm certain you know about artificial limbs ... Tom. What we're trying to do here is build better ones than can be manufactured on Earth. Because of the null-gravity capability, we don't have to machine parts. We can cast them, and they can be much lighter."

Tom was pleased; Anita was opening up. Even her voice had less of an edge to it. He wanted to know more about her. "Oh, yes, cyborgs. I've always been interested in ... that ..."

Instantly, Tom knew he had made some kind of horrendous mistake, but he didn't know what it was. Anita's face turned white and then bright red. She sat stiffly, unmoving for a moment. When she looked at him, her eyes were cold. That wall of ice, Tom realized, was back, and thicker than ever.

Leaning down, Anita pulled up the right leg of her jumpsuit. In spite of himself, Tom gasped. From just below the knee down, her leg was artificial, a smooth plastic housing around an intricately woven mass of wires and computer memory modules, powerful batteries with an external recharging plug, and some metal struts.

"I guess you could say I am something of an expert on the subject, Mister Swift!" She let the pants leg drop and turned back to her television screen, which showed, greatly magnified, a section of the device she was working on.

Tom didn't know what to say at first. "But you played null-gravity handball so well!" He knew he was sticking his foot farther and farther into his mouth, but he couldn't help himself. Then suddenly he was angry. Anita had deliberately and savagely plunged in for the kill—at her own expense—just to leave him looking foolish and feeling insensitive.

"Does it give you some sort of ghoulish thrill to shock people that way, Anita?"

Tom could see her mouth compress into a hard line, but before either could say more, Mark Scott came in. He was carrying the module of some electronic device that Tom did not recognize.

"Sorry I took so long on this, Anita, but— Oh, Mister Swift." He looked from one to the other, sensing some kind of problem.

Anita turned briskly away from her workbench and took the module from Mark, examining it closely as she talked. "That's all right, Mark. I'm sure you did a good job. This module must be perfect . . . if the *Valkyrie* is to win the Space

Triangle Race!" She looked up suddenly, staring right into Tom's eyes, and he knew he had been strongly challenged.

Anita set the module on her workbench and opened a side panel to reveal the array of delicately printed circuitry cards. She rolled up her right sleeve, exposing what appeared to be a very elaborate and expensive wristwatch. It had the usual LED crystal face, but it was larger than normal, with a surrounding display of buttons in various colors.

Tom watched in silent fascination as Anita punched out a code. A green light came on. Then she ran another series of numbers, and a light appeared within the module Mark had brought in. Anita glanced at Tom, but there was no humor in her smile.

"Biomechanoids in space, Mister Swift! That has a nice ring to it, doesn't it? Like a movie. We can perform some remarkable technical feats, you know. All of us cyborgs—"

"Stop it, Anita." Mark Scott interrupted, putting a hand on her shoulder.

Anita patted the hand absently and looked again at Tom. "I'm quite all right, Mark. I was just trying to explain to young Mister Swift the many uses to which I can put my whizbang peg-leg here! You see, Mister Swift, it has extensive computer capabilities. Even as we speak, I'm testing for electrical circuit continuity in this control-panel module. My wrist controller is connected by an ultrathin wire right through the main artery in my leg, up my side and out my arm. That's why I wear this on the same side as my pegleg. You see, it's doing the testing."

She wiggled her leg. "I can give you the latest market reports, up-to-the-minute baseball scores, anything. If it isn't in storage here, it contacts the colony computer and that marvelous gizmo can talk to any computer of note on Earth or the Moon! Isn't that remarkable? A live-in extra brain—"

"Anita!"

"Oh, shut up, Mark! I'm not finished with my pitch for human machines in space, yet. Mister Swift expressed a specific interest in cyborgs, and I'm just trying to satisfy his curiosity."

Anita's gaze bored into Tom's. "You asked me how I could play null-gravity ball so well, so I'll tell you. My own leg is connected neurally to my artificial leg. Nerve impulses are converted to electrical impulses, and the leg responds naturally. There are sensors on the heel, the ball of the foot, the toes; they give feedback. When there's a malfunction it feels like I've stepped on a tack or I'm being tickled or I have a hotfoot. Isn't science wonderful, Mister Swift?"

Tom knew that the redhead was quietly battering him with all the verbal force she could muster. She wanted to break him, to goad him into humiliating himself in some way that would give her satisfaction. He sensed the bitterness behind it and wondered about its cause. He knew many people had been injured in space before they learned how to maneuver. Limbs and sight had been lost, organs injured or destroyed. But with worldwide computerized control and the commonly accepted habit of organ donation, much of the suffering was avoided.

Tom had never met anyone with such venomous self-hatred. Anita was a beautiful young woman, and Tom had found himself attracted to her, on several levels, from the very first moment. But now, her delicate features were so distorted by self-pitying rage that he had difficulty defending himself again. The only way he could fight back was by not letting Anita see the real effect she was having on him. He sensed she would stick a verbal knife right into any perceived weakness.

Abruptly, Anita turned back to the workbench, punching savagely at the buttons on her wrist device. She smiled, and Tom thought it was a genuine smile of pleasure. "The module checks out, Mark. It's perfect. You're a wonder. Thanks!"

Mark smiled nervously, looked from Anita to Tom, and walked to the lab door. "I'll talk to you later, Anita," he said. "How about dinner tonight? Jumper is testing his new protein steak on us."

"Sure, Mark," she said. "I just hope it isn't like his lamb substitute. About seven, eh?"

Mark waved and left, and Anita turned back to the bench. She shoved the module aside and returned to examining the magnified screen image. She punched a few buttons on the console, and the image jumped from 100X to 500X. Without looking at Tom, she said, "And now you'll have to excuse me, Mister Swift, I have work to do."

"Anita, I—"

She looked at him. "If you want to beat me, you better get to work, too, don't you think?" She turned back to the screen. "Besides, if you stay here, someone might accuse you of pirating my designs . . . and an inventive genius like you wouldn't want to get a reputation for that, now, would he?"

There was so much Tom wanted to say to Anita at that moment, and he was frustrated because he knew it was an inappropriate time.

"No . . . he wouldn't," Tom replied. He turned and walked out of the lab.

Chapter Nine

It took more than two weeks and a lot of hard work, but Tom put together a welded-steel framework and mounted his prototype fusion drive. The new racer had a very incomplete look, as if the shell had been left off, but it was, in fact, almost finished. At this point, he just didn't have time to create a life-support unit in which he could exist without a spacesuit, or a radiation shield. Now, he was ready for his first test. It wouldn't be a long one, and he would be connected directly to the oxygen recycler. He'd be uncomfortable but in no danger, and the bare framework was made for quick assembly.

Tom had divided his energy between the mostly physical and mechanical work of putting together his racer, the *Davy Cricket,* and the after-work effort of trying to figure out what had gone wrong with Grotz's Prometheus drive in his first racer.

The *Davy Cricket* had come along quite well, but Tom's research into the Grotz space drive had not gotten anywhere. "It's as if Doctor Grotz hadn't done his homework," Tom had said to Ben. "His published test results don't match what I've done, and I can't determine where I'm wrong."

Ben had attempted, time and again, to help his friend out with the computer work, but their work seemed stymied. Either they were missing something vital—and perhaps very obvious—or they were completely on the wrong trail. Neither alternative was a pleasant one.

Now Tom was out in space, suited up and strapped into his spidery racer, about to test his prototype fusion drive. In contact with Ben in Control, he was running a long and exhaustive check of every element.

Tom was not the only one out testing a racer. A hundred miles off, in another designated test area, the *Régine* was being put through its paces. A bit farther out, the *Moonstreak, Alyson Rhonda II,* and *Sandy C* were having a little friendly race.

"Tom," Ben said over the radio.

"Yes, Ben?"

"The test area vertically below you will be

occupied soon. Doctor Greg Ellison is running a test."

"Oh?" Tom was intrigued. "Why?"

"Don't ask me, I just route 'em."

"Okay, I'll keep within my space. *Davy Cricket* out."

Dr. Hans Grotz was in his laboratory, watching an array of television monitors and readout screens. Each of them was linked to sensors aboard the test craft.

"In position, Doctor," said the young pilot, Grotz's protégé, Dr. Greg Ellison.

Grotz stared at Ellison a long moment before answering. The young man, busy flipping switches on his ship's control panel, did not notice the pause. This was it, Grotz thought. This test would decide whether he had corrected the errors in his original calculations on the stress factor of the Prometheus drive.

"Very well," Grotz said. "Begin countdown."

"Yes, sir. Starting fusion drive."

Grotz watched the numbers change and the graphs shift. The delicate sensing machine was very accurate. Everything was normal. The magnetic bottle was building, area by area, within the fusion chamber. It was perfect. Everything was on the predicted graph line. Silly of me to worry, Grotz thought.

"Ready to open bottle," Ellison said.

"Green light," Grotz muttered.

The magnetic-stability chart took a sudden jump. Nothing to worry about, Grotz thought. If the field fails, it simply collapses on itself . . . all action ceases. Not like nuclear plants, where if something goes wrong it takes a massive, expensive, and complex backup to prevent serious trouble.

No, nothing to worry about . . .

Grotz did not hear the explosion, of course, nor did young Greg Ellison. But the monitor screens went wild before they collapsed to zero.

Grotz stared with bulging eyes at what the sensors told him. *Explosion*!

"Ellison! Ellison! Greg!" Grotz clutched at the edge of the control board. "Report! Ellison!"

Nothing.

Grotz forced himself to be calm. The drive had blown up. Something was wrong. Ellison was a careful pilot, a scrupulously exact assistant. Could he have done something fatally wrong?

Grotz repeated his call, then sat back, thinking. Ellison had to be dead. Maybe it's better this way, Grotz thought. No witnesses to his failure. His conspicuous failure. He'd go over everything himself, figure out what went wrong, then fix the drive aboard the *Daniel Boone*. He'd blame the necessity for change on the technicians who installed the drive or the engineers who misread his plans. He'd use his career weight to bulldoze them. Their protests would not get back to Earth. It would be their fault, not his. He'd—

"Doc ... tor ..." There was a weak voice on the radio. Ellison's; he wasn't dead. Grotz stared. There was another sound, a groan, then silence.

Ellison was alive.

He couldn't be alive.

Grotz swallowed thickly. He shouldn't be alive.

Grotz suddenly felt hatred. Ellison was alive, spoiling all his plans, spoiling the story he would tell.

Die! Grotz thought venomously.

There was no sound from the radio.

"*Davy Cricket*, this is Control."

"Yes, Control, this is *Davy Cricket*."

"Did you see anything below you?" Ben asked. "Doctor Ellison's test vehicle went off the screen. Radar says they are not malfunctioning."

"Any distress signals?" Tom was already scanning the area below him. He turned his craft on control jets and checked his radar screen. Nothing.

"No, nothing," Ben said. "Listen, I've called Doctor Grotz, but there's no answer in his lab."

"Want me to go see?" Tom asked.

"Would you? We can use it to test while we're at it."

"Sure. Okay, firing up."

"Good luck."

Tom laughed. "Luck can replace skill, all right . . . but only so many times."

The fusion reaction started. Tom hesitated only a second before he thumbed the switch that would open the magnetic bottle a fraction of an inch.

A wire-thin string of fire issued from the rear of the racer, and the stars began to move around him. Tom smiled. It worked!

The racer itself didn't seem to move. It was the stars and the distant *New America* that seemed to shift. Tom moved south of the plane determined by the axis of the space colony, his eyes going from the radar's image to the blackness ahead.

"Anything?" Ben asked.

"Not yet. I . . . Wait!" From the corner of his eye, Tom saw a flash of light reflected from something going past a few hundred yards away. It was only a quick flash, but Tom watched the area and saw it again, then again a few moments later. It was a fragment of metal, rotating, catching the light of the Sun. Tom followed the path back in his mind and began searching the area from which the shard had come.

"Ben! Ben, I see something. Yes, it's on radar. It's . . . it looks like . . . yes, it's some kind of wreck, a . . . a . . ." Tom strained his eyes. "I think there's a man there. Looks like a yellow spacesuit."

"That's him, Tom! Greg has a canary-yellow suit, I know it well."

"I'm closing. Reversing jets. Slowing down. Yes . . . yes, I can see him now. He's hurt, Ben."

"Get him in here, Tom, quick!"

"Closing . . . too busy to talk right now . . ."

"I understand, Tom."

Tom cut his jets and drifted closer, making only small maneuvering movements. The man in the yellow spacesuit was belted to the twisted wreck of something mechanical. Parts were drifting about. The entire stern of the small craft was gone, and the midship section was a torn shambles.

Tom fired his reverse jets and came to a virtual stop next to the wreckage. He snapped a safety line to the framework of his vessel and then to himself. He unbelted and pushed free of the seat, kicking off toward Greg Ellison.

Hans Grotz burst through the door of his office, out of breath and perspiring heavily. He jerked open his desk drawer and fumbled for the special key to his console. He activated the console and then typed out a simple message in a code that he had worked out especially for his communications with his "errand boys," Worden and Deckert. The two power-hungry thugs loved their work, and Grotz always made sure that their imaginations were kept properly stimulated, by making their assignments as much like games of "secret agent" as possible.

He had never asked them to kill for him before. He knew they would want a lot of monetary compensation for that. He would pay it gladly and then . . . well, accidents can happen to everyone in space. Handle one crisis at a time, he told himself. Right now, Dr. Greg Ellison could not live. Grotz was sorry to be losing such a valuable and loyal employee, but having Ellison around to tell tales just wasn't in Grotz's game plan. With a sigh of relief, the scientist pressed a button on the console and beamed the coded message to the *Régine*.

Tom could see that something had crushed in the rear portion of Ellison's life support system. Looking through the plastic dome, Tom saw that the young man was bleeding and unconscious. He also saw something else that made his blood freeze. Beyond Ellison's still, floating form, he could make out a slender, silver object heading straight for the wreckage. It was a ship, and it was on a collision course with the wreckage—and with him!

Chapter Ten

In the cockpit of the *Régine,* it was Dan Deckert who spotted Tom Swift first. "Chet! That's the *Davy Cricket!* Grotz didn't say anything about Tom Swift being here!"

"He sure didn't," answered Chet Worden. "I don't see any way to carry out orders now that we've got a witness. We could have taken care of Ellison quietly and called it an accident, but killing Tom Swift too—that's another thing!"

"I'm not going to chance it, Chet," Deckert said firmly. "It's just too risky!"

"Let's pull out."

Floating in space, next to the injured Greg Ellison, Tom was relieved to see the small silver ship veer suddenly and head off at a sharp angle, and he quickly focused all his attention on the injured pilot.

Tom unbelted Ellison and hooked a short line to the unconscious pilot's belt. Then he kicked off, sending the wrecked ship tumbling away, and pulled both of them, hand over hand, to the *Davy Cricket*. He strapped Ellison into the rear and spun the tiny racer around in a spurt of flaming energy.

"Coming in with Ellison," Tom said. "Will land at the southern dock—have a medical team ready. He's hurt badly!"

"We'll have some medics in suits outside by the time you arrive, Tom," Ben said. "Keep comin'."

Tom disengaged his helmet and lifted it off as he watched the medics hustle the injured pilot away, swimming in the gravityless chamber. Their stretcher had a complex life support system built in. Sensors were already attached to slits cut in Ellison's suit.

Tom saw Ben coming through a hatch.

"How is he?" Ben asked.

Tom shrugged. "Bad. One of the medics thought he'd need some surgery—maybe a lung replacement."

Ben shook his head sadly. "That's rough. I don't care if he was Grotz's right-hand man, it's too bad."

Tom's eyes narrowed in determination. "And what, I wonder, does Grotz have to say about this?"

Ben looked embarrassed. "Ah, we got hold of him. He, uh, he says Ellison was conducting unauthorized experiments."

"So, it's all Greg's fault, huh?"

Ben shrugged. "Looks that way."

Tom frowned and struck the bulkhead with his balled fist. The motion made him swing around and move backward toward the opposite side.

"Ben, we've got to do something about Grotz!"

"The race will commence here, at *New America,* on the twenty-second, at 01:00 Greenwich Time," said the official from United Nations Near-Space Traffic Control. "You will be precisely positioned by radar from here and will start, by lot, in staggered release. Traffic lanes have been cleared from *New America* to *Sunflower.*"

The man in the gray jumpsuit looked from one to another of the assembled racers and sponsors in the room. "Remember, you must approach *Sunflower* within the designated cone of space perpendicular to its plane of rotation. This is to test not only the speed of your craft, but also its safety, navigability, and maneuverability, all of which are necessary in any spaceworthy vessel."

Ben stirred restlessly, uncomfortable at the news briefing called to announce the rules and terms of the race. He looked at the news cameras nearby and wondered just how much of this would actually be rebroadcast to Earth. Although it was the first race of its kind, the details were very well known all over the globe. There were three Russian and two Japanese entries, one Chinese and two French—including the renowned Philippe Yost—as well as English, Canadian, Swedish, Mexican, and Ceylonese entries. It was going to be a crowded sky.

Ben looked at Tom, studying him. His friend from Earth had that faraway look of someone studying a problem in his mind. It was obvious Tom was paying only token attention to the ceremony.

"From *Sunflower* you must make a physical touchdown at Armstrong Base on the Moon, then you must return to *New America* through the *designated* corridors of passage, which will not be direct, but will again require navigational factors."

"Wow," a voice in the crowd spoke up, "that's gonna be about six days' worth o' flyin'!"

The official ignored the interruption. "We are duly grateful for the representation that has been shown here, from the technologically advanced nations, and from interested young people. Ladies and gentlemen, I wish you luck!"

The lights from the cameras died, then brightened again sporadically as various newsmen took individual portraits of the young racers. Tom seemed to awake with a start and took Ben's elbow.

"Come on, let's get out of here."

"Mister Swift! Tom!" Tom saw a newswoman pushing her way through the crowd, towing a cameraman behind her.

"Uh-oh," Tom muttered.

"Mister Swift, I'm Michele Kurland, Global News."

"Yes, ma'am?"

"Are you still in the race after your accident? Will you get your star drive ready in time?"

"It's hardly a star drive, Miss Kurland. The distance to even the nearest star is four years at light speed—186,600 miles per second."

"Yes, yes, but you're the underdog now, Mister Swift. Your craft is still in testing while these others are operational."

"Just let me say, ma'am, that we will try our best. Now you'll have to excuse me."

"Yes, but—"

When Tom saw another news team looking at him, he ducked away, followed by Ben. They gained the corridor and slipped through a passage as the noise died down behind them.

When they had slowed down, Ben said, "Why were you so abrupt?"

Tom shrugged. "I really don't like to talk about things before they are complete. We still have a lot of work to do. It's less important that I finish the racer than it is to find out what's wrong with Grotz's drive."

Ben nodded. "Yeah, you're right. But that was the first time I've been on that kind of TV." He grinned sheepishly. "It's pretty wild. To think my uncle Fire Cloud or my cousin Star Flower might have seen me."

"Fire Cloud?"

"My grandparents saw an atomic explosion. That's a lot more impressive than a running bear or a sitting bull—or a walking eagle!"

Tom laughed and said, "Well, it certainly is more colorful than Bill or Harry or Elizabeth."

"Or Tom," Ben kidded.

Tom pretended indignation, and then they laughed together. "C'mon," Tom said. "We've got work to do. Which reminds me, Ben. You will join me during the race as my copilot, won't you?"

Ben grinned and slapped his buddy on the shoulder. "Will I? Just try keeping me away!"

In his office, Dr. Hans Grotz stared moodily at the figures on the screen. This mess was all young Swift's fault. How dare Swift put his nose in *his* business. The voice of his conscience tried to soothe him. He knew he was where he was because he wasn't afraid to seize the moment. He followed his intuition—something all the greats of science did. So what if he didn't always check things out to the tenth decimal point, he was always right, wasn't he? He had fudged on tests before. This time, he had been caught, that's all. It made things a little harder, but he could handle it.

Grotz chewed at his lower lip, his brows knitted. He had made fast decisions, and that was one of the reasons he was acting director of the greatest construction made by man. Besides, he had always been able to blame mistakes on others—Evans, Hayworth, poor suicidal Bailey, the de Toledo woman. He had covered up before, and he would cover this one up. Better get to it!

He would start by complaining to Congress, NASA, and the media that Swift Enterprises was cost-cutting and not following specifications. At first, just some off-the-record comments, then a few on-record remarks, carefully worded, of course. Tom Swift would get blamed—and his father as well. Even if Grotz somehow were blamed, confidence in Swift Enterprises would be so eroded that what he had done would seem insignificant compared with the crimes of the "corporate monster." Young Swift and his father would be badly hurt. Grotz began to chuckle to himself. It was very good! He couldn't lose that way. If he did find the flaw in his own calculations, he could still be the hero and Swift Enterprises would still be hurt. They would be blamed for interfering with his work!

He would have to alter certain facts, however. The paper work was no problem; everything was still in computer storage. Grotz smiled to himself. He was an expert at computer retrieval, and no code was really safe from him. He'd pull the basic plans, alter them, maybe make it look as though computer error or incorrect input by the operators had caused the problem.

Actually, even if the *Daniel Boone* didn't make it, he would be safe. Of course, he wouldn't go on the maiden voyage now. Not even the test flight. He would have to think of some excuse. Perhaps grief at Ellison's death.

Ah yes, Dr. Greg Ellison. It was too bad Worden and Deckert had lost their nerve on that job. They'd signed their own death warrants for that. But he would deal with them later. Greg Ellison wasn't dead yet, but it was only a matter of time. His spine was injured, he had a bad concussion, and there was extensive damage to his internal organs. They had already transplanted a kidney, and an artificial heart was coming up on the next shuttle. The boy wouldn't make it. He couldn't make it; that would ruin everything! It had been with Ellison's help that he had falsified a few records on the peripheral testing. The boy had been so blinded by the reputation of the older man, he had actually believed it was all right.

No, the boy couldn't live—even if *he* had to insure it.

He had to get young Swift off his back, too. His own private alarm code on all his computerized plans told him whenever someone had tapped them, and Tom and Ben Walking Eagle had been calling for more and more test results. Sooner or later, the upstarts might find out what was wrong. That mustn't happen. Something must be done about Swift and his friend.

Grotz swiveled to check his computer console. Did Tom and Ben really know what they were facing in an adversary like himself? The big man chewed his lower lip thoughtfully, then he began rapidly punching buttons on the console, all the while chuckling to himself.

It was funny how, in the last few hours, he had begun to think of murder as a viable tool in the shaping of his destiny. It felt so natural, so right.

After a few moments, he grunted with satisfaction and shut down the console. "Wilma," he said into the intercom, "tell Worden and

Deckert that they'll be working . . . er . . . late tonight and to come see me in the lab after ten o'clock."

"Yes, Doctor. I . . . I'm so sorry about Doctor Ellison, sir. We . . . we all loved him."

Dr. Grotz swung around in his chair, a satisfied smile on his face. It was all so easy, he thought. Why hadn't he considered murder before? Not murder, he corrected himself. It was so much nicer to call it an accident. An accident in space. And it was so easy to arrange!

So much for Tom Swift and his friend Ben Walking Eagle. They would never know they were in danger until it was too late to do anything about it. Grotz laughed out loud. He knew exactly what kind of accident the two boys would have—and very soon!

Chapter Eleven

The light blinked on the communication panel
and Tom Swift punched a HOLD on his calculations, switching the screen over to Telecommunications.

"Hello, Son."

"Dad!" Tom leaned forward eagerly. "I've
been trying to get hold of you!"

"I know, I'm sorry. But Triton Dome had a
serious problem. An unsuspected fault in the
ocean floor cracked the outer dome. There was
considerable flooding. The thermal-differential
power plant was put out of commission, and
we had to patch-in a fusion plant." The tall,
gray-haired man smiled at his son. "It's done
with now. They're mopping up—literally—and

113

things are getting back to normal. What's going on up there? You had an accident I heard, but they said you were all right."

"Dad, you've got to stop the drive installation on the *Daniel Boone*."

The older man looked very serious. "Why, Son? We have a contract with a tight deadline, you know."

Quickly, Tom outlined what had happened and what he thought was wrong, as well as certain things he labeled rumors and suspicions. "But what I can't figure out is why Doctor Grotz was down on me from the first time I met him. Before that, even!"

The distinguished elder Swift nodded soberly. "I do. It goes back quite a few years, Tom. Before you were born, in fact. Hans Grotz was the bright star among the younger scientists then. We were both working on the solution to a specific problem which was vital for a hush-hush spy satellite system. We came up with different ways to handle it and because my alternative was much less expensive, it was accepted by the government."

"I see." Tom said. "There was some rivalry between you two."

"That's right and a lot of jealousy on Grotz's part. He tried to discredit my work, but didn't get anywhere."

"But I can't understand why he would still

bear a grudge so many years later." Tom said. "After all, now he has a reputation of a brilliant scientist in his own right and . . ."

"Well, there was something else." Mr Swift admitted. "I was dating your mother at the time and Grotz fell in love with her. Again he lost out in the competition and was rejected. I think that's the one thing he'll never forget or forgive me for."

Tom looked at his father a moment. "So he hates me because he hates you."

The elder Swift looked at his son soberly. "Maybe you better drop out of that race, Tom. I know Hans Grotz. He's . . . he's capable of anything."

Tom shook his head. "No, Dad, I can't. I'm too close to figuring out what's wrong. I know it." Tom held up a thumb and forefinger a fraction of an inch apart. "There's something obvious here that I'm not seeing, I think."

Tom's father smiled again. "Not seeing the obvious has delayed many an invention, Son. Well, I should know better than to try to get you to back away from something. You watch yourself, now."

Tom smiled at his father and they said goodbye. He sat back and then became aware that Ben was in the doorway behind him. "Oh, Ben . . ." But Ben was staring past him, transfixed. Tom turned to see what Ben was looking at and gasped. A computer image of a duck was walking back and forth across the console screen.

Tom stepped aside just in time to avoid a collision as the computer technician rushed passed him. "What happened, Ben?" Tom asked. He had never seen his friend so upset. But Ben did not answer. His attention was riveted on the keyboard of his console. Ben rapidly punched a sequence of numbers and letters, then watched the screen in tense silence. Three more ducks joined the first.

"Ben . . . ?"

"I've been robbed," Ben said softly, not taking his eyes from the console screen. "Someone has entered my console on a remote and scrambled my personal information bank—someone very, very good! I have an awful feeling that it's going to take me a long time to straighten it out."

"Who would have the—"

"There's only one person in *New America* with that kind of power and the ability to use it, Tom, and this was his warning to us."

"Grotz. He doesn't like our investigation."

"Uh-huh." Ben switched the console off. "I don't want to attempt to reprogram, now. I'll need a clear head when I try to sort this thing out."

"It must have happened while I was talking to my father," Tom said. "Don't worry, we'll work this out."

Both boys sat quietly, thinking about all that

had happened and how all the pieces fit together. Suddenly Tom slapped a hand down on the table. "I say we give the ol' *Davy Cricket* a burn test tomorrow! What do you say?"

"Both of us?"

"Sure, you're not backing out of your duties as copilot, are you?"

Ben grinned and jumped up. "I wouldn't miss the test for anything. We'll burn up the skies!"

Both young men laughed, for a "burn test" was a slang engineering term. You designed something, built it, and then you plugged it in and turned it on. If it started smoking, it didn't pass the burn test.

Hans Grotz entered the lab and immediately locked the door. He paused only long enough to get a pair of heavy safety glasses and put them on. He made his way through the maze of tables laden with electronics-testing equipment until he reached the laser. He had been familiarizing himself with the adjustments of the small table laser for just a few minutes when he heard a soft knock at the lab door. Worden and Deckert were earlier than he thought they'd be. That was good. They'd had no trouble pulling the electronic slab from the *Davy Cricket*'s computer, then.

His two henchmen entered the lab, smirking with satisfaction.

"Where is it?" Grotz asked tensely.

Dan Deckert held out his hand and Grotz carefully took the delicate printed circuit slab. The scientist held it up to the light for examination. It was a plastic panel just thick enough to be rigid, with a complex layering of photographically reduced diagrams printed on it. The patterns were separated by layers of insulation with holes in them to connect the electronics. It was an immensely complex, but fairly standard piece of machinery for that time. The modular system was perfect for replacement procedures.

"Amuse yourselves for a while, gentlemen," Grotz mumbled, "and then I want you to replace this exactly where you found it."

"*Davy Cricket* to Control, we are leaving the corridor for test area seven," Tom said.

"Roger, *Cricket*. Eight and eleven are occupied, so check your radar."

"Roger. *Cricket* out."

Tom glanced at Ben sitting in the copilot's seat of the spidery craft, suited up and smiling. They were moving through the monitored traffic lanes on steering jets of air. Tom's use of his fusion drive to rescue Greg Ellison had only been condoned because of the emergency nature of the operation.

"Well, are you ready, buddy?" Tom asked via the suit's radio. This was to be the first test of the delicate attitude controls that would give the small craft the necessary maneuvering power. Tom's previous use of the fusion drive had been like driving a tractor, compared to the racing-car maneuverability he expected to get with the added controls.

Ben nodded and Tom touched the console before him, his gloved fingers pressing the large buttons.

The drive flared behind them, and the craft moved ahead at once. Tom ran his eyes over the console. Everything was fine. Then he reached for the attitude control stick which would angle the jet, moving the craft up, down, or sideways.

It did not respond.

Quickly, Tom pressed the drive-shutdown switch.

It didn't work.

They were heading into space in a craft they could neither stop nor control!

"*New America* Control, this is *Davy Cricket*," Tom said, keeping his voice calm. As he spoke Tom was thumbing the distress signal that would transmit on another frequency.

"Come in, *Cricket*."

"Trouble here. Controls jammed. Under maximum thrust and"—Tom looked at the navigation display to give the exact position and flight path—"we're passing through section eight, going for Pluto." It was a weak joke. He looked at Ben, but the dark-haired copilot was already unstrapped and wriggling through the struts to inspect the fusion drive.

Ben stuck his head around the radiation shield and looked the mechanical linkages over. The electrical connections were less easily seen.

"It must be in the wiring, Tom, or in the computer itself."

Tom looked over his shoulder. The massive cylinder of the space colony was shrinking behind them. Tom bent and looked closely at the on-board computer between the seats. This was the brain of the spacecraft, Tom's own design, based on the Swift production-line Newton model popular in many small spacecraft, but with some features added by Tom.

As Ben struggled back into his seat, Tom ran a status check, his fingers busy on the computer console and his eyes on the readout screen.

"It says everything is all right," Tom muttered.

"Computers never lie," Ben said. "But sometimes they don't know it's a lie. Let me at that— this is my territory."

"*Cricket,* we don't have anything that can catch you," *New America* Control said. "You're built too well. We've diverted the *Elie Metchnikoff* from test area fifteen, but I think you have too much of a start on them."

"Understand, Control. We'll handle it at this end."

"You sound awfully confident," Ben muttered.

"Well, I have you, don't I, ol' Walking Eagle?" Tom said lightly. He twisted in his seat and looked back at the flaming jet from the fusion plant. He tried again to slow their reckless outward velocity with the braking and steering jets, but they, too, were malfunctioning.

"Tom, I think someone's reprogrammed your computer," Ben said. "The computer took the order to fire and is rejecting all other orders." He looked up at Tom, the instrument light reflecting off the metallic glass of his space helmet. "I told you these things were dumb."

"It rejects all override and reprogramming attempts?"

"Yup. This is going to take a while."

"*Cricket,* this is *New America* Control. The *Metchnikoff* reports unable to overtake you. The *Starlightning* is vectoring in from area twenty-three and has you on visual."

Tom looked around in the sky and found the tiny moving dot of light that was the other racer. "*Starlightning,* this is *Davy Cricket,* over."

"*Cricket,* I can see you, but man! you are traveling!"

Tom realized that the other racer was not going to be able to match their speed. "*Starlight-

ning, forget it. You're a chemical rocket, right?"

"Affirmative . . . and there's not much fuel left, I'm afraid."

"Abort, *Starlightning,* no use two of us blowing it."

There was a pause, and the other pilot said, "Understand, *Cricket.* Sorry. *Starlightning* out."

Ben looked at Tom. "How much time do we have before we run out of fuel?"

Tom smiled wanly. "Six days. We'd be halfway to the asteroid belt by then."

"Marvelous," Ben muttered. He bent over the computer again. "Well, partner, I'm going to have to do serious damage to your electrical brain here. I'm going to give it amnesia."

"Don't you want to go to the asteroids, Ben?" Tom said, keeping his tone light. Six days of continuous acceleration and then nothing could stop them. They'd just keep going. A hundred million years or so later some alien life form might see them zipping through its star system and collect them as a relic.

"Yes, I'd like to go to the asteroids," Ben grunted, bent over awkwardly, prying loose the computer cover. "But I forgot my camera. Never go . . . anywhere . . . without . . . my . . . camera," Ben said slowly, his eyes and fingers tracing the identification numbers. His gloved hand reached down and pulled a printed circuit slab from the heart of the computer.

Instantly the fusion plant ceased working. The *Cricket* kept going straight ahead, of course, but now it would not continue to build acceleration.

"There, it's forgotten every order given it," Ben said.

"Let me see that," Tom said. He examined the complex printed slab carefully, then pointed. "There. It's been altered."

"How do you do that?" Ben asked in some amazement. "The darn things are printed photographically in vacuum and sealed in plastic."

Tom pointed. "A laser drilled two holes at these points, and a jumper line was established. Look. If I didn't know this computer as well as I do, I wouldn't notice it."

"Great. Now we have a computer with no memory and no way to fix it."

"Sure we do," Tom said. "We send it to kindergarten. It'll still work. It just doesn't know what to do."

"Of course," Ben exlaimed. "My suit radio. We can patch through to the station computer, and someone there can give our little dumbbell a new memory, routing around the sabotaged area and—"

Ben stopped. He and Tom looked at each other for a moment. It sank in all at once. They had been sabotaged! Someone had tampered with the on-board computer.

Someone had tried to kill them!

Chapter Twelve

Back on *New America* that evening, Tom and Ben looked at the screen over the workbench. The microcamera was poised over the sabotaged circuit board, and they could clearly see the lasered hole and the almost microscopic line that had been laid down to short it out. They also found a microprocessor chip imbedded in the plastic.

"The Newton line is common enough," Tom explained. "Someone just took a slab and worked it over and substituted his for ours."

"Or hers," Ben suggested.

"Hers? You mean, uh, Anita might have done this?" Tom was truly surprised. "She doesn't seem the type."

"Tom, maybe you don't know what this race

has come to mean. It's focusing a lot of attention on *New America*. You know how it is; you could come up with the greatest scientific discovery of the century, and it wouldn't get as much attention as the time that ballplayer hit a baseball the whole three-mile length of the null-gravity axis. The race will make the winner famous, it'll even make the losers a little famous! And, most importantly, it'll insure the winners a berth on the *Daniel Boone* when it goes out." Ben paused, switching off the microcamera. "There are people up here who are ambitious, maybe ambitious enough to do . . . anything they thought necessary."

"Are you saying Anita did this?"

"No, not really, but don't think just 'he.' It might be 'she,' that's all."

Tom sat back and sighed. Ben picked up the slab and slipped it into a zippered pocket on his blue jumper.

"We still haven't found out what's wrong with Grotz's drive," Tom reminded his friend.

"Maybe there is nothing wrong, Tom. Maybe what happened to you and to poor Greg was, well, really an accident. Not a design flaw at all but . . . whatever: pilot error, a malfunctioning gizmo, poor quality control somewhere along the line."

"You believe that?" Tom asked.

Ben shrugged. "No, not really, but it's a possibility. Maybe we are hunting ghosts, seeing evil where there is none."

"Yes, it's a possibility," Tom admitted. "But so is the tooth fairy."

"Well, let's relax. Forget Grotz, forget the race. Let's just go have some fun tonight, what do you say?"

Tom sighed, picked up the new circuit board, and put it carefully into a pocket. "I'll feel guilty. We should be trying to get this straight."

"Feel guilty, but have some fun, too. All work and no play makes Ben a dull boy."

Tom grinned. "Okay, Ben, what do you have in mind?"

"The Aquarium." At Tom's questioning look Ben smiled and said, "It's near the center of our north end. Gravity's about five percent of normal, and we dance there."

"Dance? In that little gravity?"

"Well, it's kind of a cross between dancing, swimming, and gymnastics." At Tom's expression, Ben laughed. "I thought you might like the gymnastics part. Let's go get cleaned up. The place will be filling up in an hour."

"Sounds great, but we'd better make it an early evening. We've got the test drive to *Sunflower* first thing in the morning!"

The doughnut-shaped *Sunflower* colony spun against the stars ahead. Tom peered through his space helmet, admiring the marvelous sight. Although the *Sunflower* was still in the construction phase with whole sections unfinished, it was already beautiful.

The doughnut's hole was pierced by a long and complex construction of spheres, tanks, cylinders, bulbous labs, and machinery. This was the axis, connected to the ring by four strong tubes. At one end was a large spaceship-docking facility and at the other the spherical astronomical observatory. At the axis, a counterrotation could be maintained, making the observatory and the cargo dock "motionless" in relationship to the rest of the mile-diameter colony.

The people and the farms and factories were on the inside of the tube, which was a torus. Their "down" was the outside of the revolving doughnut and "up" was toward the mast that pierced the center. While not as big as *New America*, the new space colony would still be able to support over 40,000 people. This design was just a different response to the problem of a self-sufficient colony in space.

Eventually, there would be an enormous mylar mirror constructed "over" the mile-wide tube wheel, reflecting sunlight into the colony and maintaining the twenty-four-hour cycle.

To keep everything properly balanced, construction had proceeded on a symmetrical basis, the center complex constructed first, then the spokes and the "inner-tube" framing. Now, only four areas were left to enclose, in equal quarters. It was in one of these sections, amid thin struts of metal, that Ben's father worked.

"Come in just as the race plan says," Ben cautioned his companion. "We might as well get the practice."

"Right. *Sunflower* Control, this is the *Davy Cricket* on training flight from *New America*. Request permission to dock."

"We have you on the screen, *Davy Cricket*. Hold your position, we have a ship leaving."

"Roger, Control." Tom and Ben watched as a stubby shuttle backed out of the docking bay on airjets and floated into a clear space. Other short maneuvering bursts turned the ship around, and a small thrust from the main engines sent the craft on its way back to Earth.

Tom and Ben watched the ship leave, seeing the fiery burst of the rocket as it made a second positioning move.

"The days of chemical rockets are just about gone, huh, Tom? Once you prove that what's back there works," Ben said, aiming a thumb to the stern, "we'll start a whole new era."

"Once *we* prove it out," Tom said. "Don't

forget there are a lot of people working on a fusion drive."

"Yes, and a lot of people were working on powered flight at the beginning of the twentieth century, too—but a pair of brothers are the ones that did it."

"I'm no Wright brother, Ben, and—"

"*Cricket*, this is *Sunflower* Control. Get ready for docking."

"Roger, *Sunflower* Control."

Chet Worden and Dan Deckert were in the docking bay. The name of their ship, *Régine*, was hand-lettered in gaudy colors across the back of their life-support-system backpacks. Tom saw them look at him and move away, toward their own vessel. Beyond them, he saw Anita Thorwald in her apple-green spacesuit plugging an air line into her ship's oxygen tanks.

Tom grasped a handhold and moved across to her, hand over hand in the airless space. She looked up and saw him, then deliberately turned her back.

"Hello, Anita," Tom said. When she didn't respond, he pulled back his head and checked the inner rim of his helmet where the tabs told what frequency he was broadcasting on. No, he was on the commonly used suit-to-suit line. "Anita?" She climbed stiffly into her ship and released the magnetic grapple. Almost at once her steering jets flared air, which turned at once into a cone of ice crystals. Her *Valkyrie* backed out and was quickly lost in the void beyond.

Tom stared after her. Why had she so deliberately snubbed him? He shrugged and floated back past Worden and Deckert and pulled himself into the *Davy Cricket*. It was only then he noticed how still Ben was. "What is it?"

Ben pointed silently at the control console. "Don't touch that starter button."

"Why?"

"Because it's been shorted." He held up a small piece of resin-core solder. "I saw this when I got in, floating just under the edge of the console, so I searched around under there. Someone fused the activation control to the steering jets. If we had started up, we would have burned out the whole mess—computer and all."

Tom sat still for a moment. "Same person as before, or what?"

"This is crude. Hasty. The other attempt was quite sophisticated." Ben looked over at Deckert and Worden. "They had the time, while we were inside. So did Thorwald."

Tom didn't know what to say. A second sabotage attempt. The stakes were getting high. And they'd caught this one only by luck. They probably wouldn't have been injured, but their finely tuned, highly complex racer would have been out of the race. There wouldn't have been time to rebuild.

"I think we had better start keeping a guard on the *Cricket*," Tom said.

Ben nodded. "I have some friends who'd do it for us. We'll need our sleep." Ben stirred in his seat. "Hang on—I'll have it defused in a few minutes and then we can be on our way back home." He looked at Tom. "You think about who did it."

"And why."

"Oh, we know *why*—to keep us out of the race."

Tom nodded. "Yes, probably. But suppose it doesn't have anything to do with the race? Suppose it's something else?"

Ben looked hard at his friend. "There's only one other thing."

Tom nodded slowly. "Grotz."

"You did *what*?" screamed Dr. Grotz. Chet Worden and Dan Deckert both jumped involuntarily. They had never seen Grotz this angry.

"We . . . we thought you'd want us to do it, Doctor Grotz," said Worden, his voice quavering.

"When I want you to do something, I'll order it! I don't want any independent thinking out of you two. Is that understood?"

The men nodded and slunk out of the office. Dr. Grotz sat back and nervously ran his fingers through his hair. Worden and Deckert were beginning to be liabilities.

The next day, Tom and Ben undertook the final test of their racer.

The *Cricket* moved smoothly out from *New America* into the testing space far from the traffic areas that were the vital links to Earth, the Moon, and the other satellites in orbit. This was to be a series of involved maneuvers that required considerable space, so *New America* was only a tiny blip on their radar.

"*New America* Control, this is *Davy Cricket*. We are entering test area forty-one. Request permission to begin tests."

"*Davy Cricket,* this is *New America* Control. Permission granted. Out."

Ben pointed, and Tom saw a slowly moving series of dots in the distance, sunlight glinting off their sides. "Ore up from the Moon," he said.

Tom nodded, and they began their maneuvers. After twenty minutes of high-speed tests that pressed the new configuration to the utmost, Tom killed the plasma jet and grinned at his companion. "Better than we thought! We can turn on a dime and give change!"

"Space travel–wise," Ben laughed. "Those turns still eat up miles!"

"Yes, but it's—"

There was an interruption on the emergency band. The characteristic piercing tone that would wake the dead preceded the urgent voice of *New America* Control. "Emergency! Solar flare! Repeat—*solar flare!* Get to cover! Emergency! Solar flare in progress!"

Ben and Tom stared at each other for a second. A solar flare was a constant hazard in space—and the most dangerous. Shielded by the atmosphere of Earth, humanity there was protected, but in the nakedness of space, there were few places to hide. One of the functions of the thick layers of soil and rock within *New America* was to act as a barrier to the deadly neutrino radiation.

"*Cricket, Woofer, Valkyrie!* Get in here!" *New America* Control said excitedly. "Get moving!"

"We're too far out," Ben said. Prolonged exposure would kill them. They had taken more than fifteen minutes to get to the test area; going back and docking would take much longer. Their little framework spacecraft did not yet have the shielding that helped protect regular ships.

There was no way to stop the flare. Unless they found some sort of shelter—and found it fast—they were doomed!

Chapter Thirteen

"*Cricket, Woofer, Valkyrie*! Do you read me?" demanded Control anxiously.

"Roger, *Woofer* coming in!"

"No, wait!" Tom cut into the babble. "*Valkyrie! Woofer*! Head for the rocks! The shipments from the Moon!"

Even as he talked Tom was wheeling the ship around on bursts of compressed air, then he thumbed the plasma jet, heading for the distant spots that swung into his radar screen.

"Understand, *Cricket*!" Tom heard Anita's voice, tense but calm. "On the way!"

"*Woofer! Woofer*, do you hear me?" Tom called.

"I'm on the way home—too late. Good luck."

Ben and Tom exchanged grim looks. *Woofer* wouldn't make it in time, for the deadly burst of radiation was coming at literally the speed of light. They had less than eight minutes before the peak of the flare arrived, but already the radiation was striking them invisibly. The very act of detection showed that the burst had arrived.

The yellow blips on the screen grew larger and separated into numerous dots as differentiation developed. "Nine ... ten ... eleven ... twelve ... thirteen," Ben counted. "I hope you're not superstitious, Tom, but thirteen packets of Moon stuff is all we have."

Tom grinned without humor. "Any port in a storm, isn't that what they say?"

"There's *Valkyrie*," Ben said, putting his gloved fingertip on the radar screen where a new dot had entered. "We're going to get there just before she does."

"Pick one," Tom said, and Ben knew just what he meant. He quickly calculated the angle which would put the most ore between them and the Sun. "That one," he said, and Tom gave the screen a quick look.

"Right. *Valkyrie*, the third shipment from the *New America* end! Got that?"

"Roger, *Cricket*!"

Tom reversed the *Cricket* and, jets flaring, he slowed down and came to a relative halt within the shadow of the massive ore shipments. Ben fired one magnetic anchor while Tom fixed the other. The group of containers floated in ghostly silence, and Tom took a look at them. There were several types. One was a bundle of nickel-iron ingots, as thick as his thigh and three times his height, held together by a magnetic cable. Six were great glass boxes made from the lunar sands and filled with metallic powder. Two were stronger, heavy-duty metal containers, ribbed and reinforced, with unidentified, more fragile cargo. Two were large chunks of unprocessed lunar ore held within lightweight nets. All of them had been fired from the surface of the Moon days before, perhaps even weeks, electrically propelled against the one-sixth gravity, and precisely aimed into an orbit that would let them end up here. These containers of ore and metal were Tom and Ben's only protection.

And Anita's. She came in, jets flaring, and almost overshot the collection of containers. She maneuvered into position, and Ben tossed her a magnetic anchor. They pulled her craft in close, and she anchored the *Valkyrie* to the metal box behind them.

No one said anything. They listened to the babble from *New America*, from the incoming shuttles, from the desperately running racers, and from Control. They sat still, unmoving and afraid. All around them, they knew, was the invisible rain of death. Nothing changed; the thirteen containers rippled and bobbed, upset by the movement the two racers had made in attaching themselves.

Tom watched the moving shadow line as the boxes bobbed. He didn't want their disturbance of the group to swing them around into the invisible fire from the sun.

They waited in silence. Solar flares usually did not last long.

"Tom?" Anita spoke up, her voice quiet.

"Yes?"

"I ... I really want to thank you. My first instinct was to run for it. I hadn't thought of coming here." She looked around, through her metallic glass helmet. "Like you, I hadn't installed a shield yet, and ... well, I want to thank you."

"No need," Tom said.

"Hey, listen," Ben exclaimed.

"*New America* Control to all spacecraft. Emergency over. Solar radiation returning to normal. Please have a medical examination at first opportunity."

On a tactical line, a *New America* operator was calling them. "*Valkyrie, Davy Cricket*—come in, please." Tom and Anita answered simultaneously. "You all right out there?"

"Affirmative," Anita replied. "We're hiding out behind the ore shipments." She looked over at Tom. "Thanks to the pilot of the *Davy Cricket.*"

Tom felt embarrassed. It was always difficult

for him to accept a compliment gracefully.

"It was obvious," he muttered.

"So are a lot of things," Ben said, "once they are pointed out. Thanks, Tom. You thought quickly. My instinct was to run, too."

"Hey, you guys, let's go back and get checked out," Tom said. "Unhook those grapples." He grinned over at Anita. "Want to race to home base?"

She looked at him across the short distance that separated their fragile-looking ships. "No . . . I'll save that for when it really counts. Then, Mister Tom Swift, I am going to beat you!"

Tom zipped up his tunic as the medic said, "You're in good health, just like your friend."

"That's a relief," Tom said. "How's Jagger?"

"The guy on the *Woofer*? Not good. His engine sheltered him a little, but he's in bad trouble. He may not make it."

Tom sighed. "Heard anything about Greg Ellison?"

"He's still in a coma. They gave him an artificial kidney and did some other tinkering, but he's bad off, too. Can't understand why he was testing without Doctor Grotz's permission."

"No, neither can I," Tom said darkly. "Well, thanks."

"That's what we're here for."

Tom went out into the corridor, where Ben

was waiting. They grinned at each other, then at Anita as she emerged from her medical inspection.

"Hi, guys. You both okay?" They nodded and she smiled. She hesitated, her smile fading, and she made a face. "Look, uh . . . I have a confession. On *Sunflower* . . . um . . . it was my fault. The trouble you had."

"Almost had," Ben said.

"Yeah . . . well, I made a mistake. I was talking to Chet and Dan. I said, well, I said I wished something would happen to you guys. I meant fate. I mean, I think I meant fate. You know, a meteorite from out of nowhere that would put you out of the race." Anita looked very uncomfortable and she ran her fingers through her thick red hair. "Those guys, they . . . well, I guess they took me seriously, they . . . did that to your console."

"Are you certain?" Tom asked.

"I heard them bragging about it." She hesitated a moment. "Look, you guys, I didn't mean for them to *do* anything. You have to believe me. I wanted . . . I wanted something to happen. Maybe you'd get discouraged, or something, but I didn't want anyone killed. And you could have been killed!"

"Ben's eagle eye saved us," Tom said, "and we'll watch out for those two in the future."

"I never liked them," Ben muttered as the

three of them walked along the corridor. "We were on the same work detail a few times. They were always thinking of ways not to pull their own weight, always had big ideas for quick money, quick fame." Ben looked hard at Anita. "And I didn't care much for you, either, hanging out with them!"

"I know, but Worden's father and my father are in business together, down on Earth. They distribute the things Thorwald Metals makes up here. And Deckert is his friend, so . . ." She looked uncomfortable and stopped near a small fountain with a graceful figure in the center. "So I was naive. I . . . I believed the things they told me about you, Tom, and you, Ben. They're good mechanics, though, good pilots, both of them. They helped me learn a lot in the races we had a few months ago. They . . ." She stopped and shrugged her shoulders. "They aren't friends, but they're more than acquaintances. There aren't all that many young people up here who share the same interests."

Anita looked at Ben. "You've been so into computers, people think you *are* one. I didn't know you liked racing."

"Tom got me interested. It's more fun than I thought."

"Fun?" Tom asked. "We've been sabotaged, almost Sun-fried, and you think it's fun? And the race hasn't even started. Fun!"

"Yeah," Ben said with a grin. "Fun."

"Fun," Tom agreed, grinning.

"I'm still going to beat you, Mister Swift," Anita said.

"Tom," Tom suggested.

"First name or last, you'll still be listed after me," Anita said, walking off with her eyebrows raised. She gave a quick wave and disappeared around the Russian consulate building.

Tom and Ben walked in the other direction, talking animatedly about just what form the shielding should take. Neither of them noticed Chet Worden and Dan Deckert step out from behind some bushes.

"Doctor Grotz will be interested in that," Deckert said, fingering his thin beard.

"Uh-huh," Worden agreed.

Deckert licked his lips nervously, but there was an eagerness in his voice. "You know, he's going to get the Nobel Prize, and he's certain to be made director. We can write our own ticket around here if we keep in with him."

"Uh-huh," Worden said. "And I don't mind doing these little bits of dirty work at all. Do you?" He grinned at his companion, who grinned back.

"Not at all! C'mon, let's find him."

They were forming up. Pilots and copilots were running last-minute checks. People were yelling, complaining, taunting, kidding, laughing. The workrooms were packed. Tom saw one of the Chinese racers sitting in impassive and immobile silence before a still-smoking computer module. Two of the members of the largest vessel, the Kingdom of Africa's *Royal Star,* were arguing. The Ceylonese and one of the Frenchmen were having tea.

Tom walked up to Ben, hunched over a computer terminal, his fingers typing madly across the keyboard. Looking over his shoulder Tom saw Ben was running comparative tests on what little they knew of Tom's fusion drive, Grotz's, and the Cal Tech research.

"Anything?" Tom asked.

Ben shot him a glance. He stabbed a finger at the numbers. "Look. Grotz is just way off here in this stress-factor area. And here." Ben cleared the screen and punched in a key code; the screen immediately built up a new set of figures. "You can see the variance is . . ." Ben caught Tom's expression and laughed. "Okay, okay, let me put it this way."

Ben's fingers played a new tune on the keyboard. The screen presented the same material in a graphic form, and Tom could easily make out the difference between the test lines. "You can see yours . . . Cal Tech . . . and . . . um . . . let's put in MIT's . . ." He pointed at the graphs.

"See, Grotz is nowhere in line, at least not along this whole stress area." Ben looked at Tom. "I think he faked it."

"Faked it?" Tom was incredulous.

"Faked it. I think he guessed. Made an approximation. Falsified the tests he didn't make. And he didn't make them in the one area, as it turns out, he should have."

"But . . . but that's so . . . so unscientific!"

"But impressive . . . if no one catches you. You look good and fast. He's probably done it before, only he wasn't caught. He wouldn't be the first scientist, in a hurry to publish, to get a grant, or to meet a deadline, that faked something."

"Well, I've heard of it, of course, but someone of Doctor Grotz's reputation . . ."

Tom turned and sat down on the bench. One of the Russians went by, glowering at Tom, and Ben grinned. "Some people just don't like competition," he said. "The Russian ships have the biggest ion drives."

"They have more than one?"

Ben nodded. "Uh-huh, three. So what? The United States has seven. There are two Japanese. It isn't the most ships, Tom, but the fastest and most maneuverable."

"And the least likely to explode."

Ben's smile faded. "I think you have the proof."

"No . . . no, I don't. I have a suspicion. Comparison charts aren't proof. But . . . hmmm . . . I think I know where to get it."

"Tom, we're going to have to take off soon." He looked at his wristwatch. "In one hour, four minutes. Hey, where you going?"

"Out."

Tom drove the electric wheelchair slowly down the hospital corridor, wandering from room entrance to room entrance. Bandaged across the lower part of his face, wearing inflatable splints on his left arm and right leg, Tom seemed every inch the bored patient in convalescence. He met a young man hobbling on a crutch who asked what had happened to him.

Tom pointed at his lower face, made a grumbling noise, and shrugged expressively. "Zigged when you should have zagged, huh?" The young man laughed. He slapped the bandaged patient on the shoulder and hobbled on. Tom hoped other people would be as fooled by his disguise.

The wheelchair rider casually drifted down the hall. He waited until there was a cluster of busy nurses at the desk before he scooted by. Then he resumed his wandering from one door to the other, looking in, reading the names posted in metal slots on each. Finally, at room 414, he stopped. He turned the wheelchair completely around, surveying the hall. Then in a quick motion, the bandaged boy backed through the door and disappeared into the room.

The room was quiet. Tom almost could not see the figure of Greg Ellison beneath the clustered machinery. Waldoes from the ceiling aimed cameras and sensors at him. Floor-based units curved up around the bed. There were tubes, a screen with a graphed pulse on it, and a carefully regulated blood transfusion.

"Greg?"

There was no sound, no motion except breathing. Tom moved closer. He didn't like hospitals. Nobody really liked hospitals, but thank heaven they were there.

"Greg? It's Tom Swift. Greg? Greg Ellison?"

Greg's eyes fluttered, then opened. His eyes seemed glazed, but slowly they moved across to look at Tom. "Swift? You're . . . you're the guy . . . who . . . saved me?"

"I helped, yes."

"What happened to you?" A feeble hand indicated Tom's condition.

"It's fake. They wouldn't let me see you. I'm here because . . . well, it's about Doctor Grotz." Tom hesitated. Maybe he was biting off more than he could chew. "Benjamin Franklin Walking Eagle and I . . . well, we think he faked a lot of tests. Do you know if he did?"

"No . . . I . . ." Greg seemed to fade away, but then he opened his eyes once again. "Wait.

There . . . was . . . something . . . I . . . I . . ."

"Take it easy."

"I suspected . . . something . . . Delta . . . look at delta . . . delta file . . . I don't believe he . . . he did it right . . ."

"Take it easy, Greg." Tom could hear heels clicking in the corridor.

"No . . . you saved . . . me. I . . . I owe you . . ."

"You don't owe me a thing. We space types have to stick together."

Two nurses came in through the door, closely followed by a short, plump doctor. "What's going on here?" the doctor snapped. "Who are you? Who's your doctor?"

Tom moved back from the bed as the nurses crowded in. "I was just looking for someone to talk to."

"Doctor Davis, his blood pressure is up," one of the nurses said. She read off the figures from the wall-mounted monitors as the doctor bent over Ellison.

Tom silently backed away, then went out the door, grateful to escape undetected.

Delta file?

Alpha, beta, gamma, delta. The fourth file? Delta what? Where should he look? Would it be the solid information he needed?

It was his only chance—and time was becoming precious!

Chapter Fourteen

"Delta?" Ben mused. He tapped out a few figures, then wiped them from the screen and began again. "Presumably it's a coded file in
Grotz's test results. Let's look at those again."
Ben closed his eyes and tilted his head for a
moment. Then he keyed a series of figures, and
the index to Grotz's results came onto the
screen.

"These are the complete data," Ben said, "not
just the published information."

"Oh, sneaky," Tom said.

"I told you a computer cannot hide its secrets
from me. It is rumored I am the seventh son
of a seventh son."

"Rumored? Who started the rumor?"

"Me. Look, a delta entry." Ben's fingers tapped again and the screen blanked, then re-built at once to a REJECT sign.

"Did he hear us coming?" asked Tom.

"I don't think so," replied the young Chero-kee. Ben leaned back in his chair, frowning in concentration. "He just planned for this kind of tampering. The bad part is that the computer can recognize all of the terminals in *New America*. I'll get through Grotz's security eventually, but he's going to know who was looking and from where. He may cause us a lot of trouble before we're ready to deal with it. It's the only thing we can do, though."

"No, it's not," said Tom, excitedly. "What if we were to tap into the computer files with a terminal that *wasn't* registered?"

"And miracles happen every day! Sure, it would be a lot faster and very private, Tom, but where . . ."

"I'll explain in a minute, Ben. I have to make a phone call."

A few minutes later, Ben was surprised to see Anita Thorwald standing at their door looking puzzled.

"The way you sounded over the phone, Tom, I thought you two guys were on the verge of being sucked out into space by a one-eyed alien! Now I see you're just hanging out! What's up?"

Tom stepped close to the beautiful redhead

and grasped her shoulders firmly, but gently. "There's no way to say this delicately, Anita, but with all that's happened to us and between us, you should know how I feel about you. Ben and I need your help. That is, we need to use your computer."

"What?" Ben said, looking from Tom to Anita, uncomprehending.

Anita blinked in surprise, then pulled up the leg of her jumpsuit, revealing her artificial leg.

"I didn't know how you'd react to my asking for this favor, but I had to ask," Tom continued. "You reacted pretty strongly when I mentioned cyborgs—"

"I'm sorry," Anita cut in. "I don't know what to say . . . except that since I met you, I've been very . . . confused. I thought I hated you, but . . . well . . . ever since Dan and Chet sabotaged your ship, I've been doing some thinking. Oh, I'm going to stop trying to say this tactfully and just say it however it comes out!

"I don't like myself very much for the things I've been thinking and doing since this whole race thing started. Sure, I want to win. I've always been ambitious and competitive; it comes from being an oldest child. My father started grooming me to take over the business practically from the crib. Nine years later, my brother was born, but it was too late to turn me back into a regular daughter."

"You don't have to explain, Anita," Tom said softly.

"I want to. When I got angry and thought I hated you for making a mistake, I was really punishing myself all over again—for a mistake I made years ago. That's how I got my leg amputated! I tried to please my father. I really did! I tried to be the best at everything to make up for . . . for being a girl. I know there's nothing wrong with a girl being ambitious and career-minded, but I wanted to be everything to my father. I had to be the first and the best. And one day, I was in too much of a hurry to beat out the competition. I had a bad accident with some machinery. I was lucky that it was only my leg that got crushed. It could have been so much worse, as it was for the technician, who saved my life. He died a few days afterward."

"Anita—"

"Let me finish, Tom! I'm looking at the inside of myself for the first time in years. I don't like what I see. I'm getting so eaten up by ambition that I'm beginning to wish doom on everybody else. I want to do something to clean out all that nastiness before it's too late. If you need my help, you've got it!"

"We're making an illegal entry into Doctor Grotz's files, Anita," Ben said after a few moments. "Just like they always do in the old movies when they secretly break into someone's office to look at their files. We're doing it with the computer, and we don't want Grotz to know who's looking just yet."

"Why, Ben?"

"Because we think Doctor Grotz is hiding some information about the *Daniel Boone*'s drive that could be critical. If we get what we're after, you'll understand the whole situation."

"Okay," Anita said, rolling up her sleeve to expose her wristband. "Does this have anything to do with the 'accident' you keep talking about, Tom?"

"Yes. This should prove whether or not what happened to my first racer was an accident after all!"

Ben began punching buttons on Anita's wristband. "Instead of going directly to the computer through a public terminal, we're going to go through your private one and catch the computer off guard." There were a few seconds of silence, and then the tiny LED crystal on the wristband began displaying some symbols.

"Aha," Ben said, almost with delight. Tom watched with growing amusement as Ben searched for the key within the key, the code sequence that would unlock the classified information.

"The thing you have to do," Ben said softly, as he watched the tiny screen and punched the buttons on the wristband, "is psych out the quarry. History professors always use historical references, almost always classical, almost always trivial. Math types use codes in codes. Politicians have code words—'Operation Bailout,' 'Operation Hideout,' rhymes, words out of their past, like their hometowns or old Army serial numbers . . ." His voice trailed off. Ben began humming tunelessly, his eyes intent on Anita's wrist screen.

"Ahh," Ben whispered.

"What is it?" Tom and Anita both asked excitedly.

"Let's put it on the big screen!" Ben punched a button on his console and pointed to the screen, which was rapidly building up an index. "He coded it under 'Bonaparte.' There's a whole bunch of things squirreled away there . . . um, look . . . there's Prometheus."

"That's the name he used for the drive," Tom said to Anita.

Ben quickly punched out the sequence, then, with Tom and Anita, he watched in fascination as the information built up in rapid letters and numbers across the screen. What they saw were the results of tests not included in the public information. Tom and Ben looked at each other. Seven of the thirteen hidden tests had not been conducted.

"He really did fake it," Ben said quietly, "a man of his reputation!"

They were silent a moment, then Tom made

a notation of the coded sequences necessary to pull the information out of the classified storage onto a readout screen.

"You know, Tom, I think this means it was Grotz who engineered your little accidents," said Ben.

"But—"

"Yes, I know, he's a reputable scientist. But he also has a lot on the line here. If you were put off, diverted into other channels, or ... killed, he'd have a clear field. He's probably been trying to find the mistakes himself."

"The test in which Greg Ellison was hurt ..." Anita broke in. "He doesn't want you or anyone else discovering those flaws. He's counting on being able to find and correct them himself."

"Over my dead body, if necessary! I'm going to have a talk with him," Tom said, straightening up.

"Maybe you'd better just turn it over to Security," Ben suggested.

Tom shook his head. "They wouldn't understand the significance of the missed tests. Grotz is still acting director of *New America*. Who do you think they'll believe, him or me? No, I've got to talk to him myself. Maybe he's found the error. Maybe everything will work out."

Ben looked disgusted. "And maybe Limburger cheese smells like roses! I say get your father, let him handle it. He knows the right people."

Again Tom shook his head. "There's so much that's just supposition on our part. He might have put the results of these tests in some other file."

"Oh, sure," Anita said wryly.

"I've got to confront him and find out the truth—"

"And then what," interrupted Anita sharply. The two young men looked openmouthed at the volatile redhead. "Do you think he'll just gladly roll over and play dead? Are you naive enough to think that he's going to turn himself in like an honorable man? He's already proved that he has no honor, so you can't expect him to play by the rules!"

"He's a scientist and an educated man. He's got too much at stake to do anything foolish."

"Yeah, and he's got too much at stake to let you ruin it," Anita said.

"At least let us go with you, Tom," Ben said.

"Thanks, but no. What you can do is try to contact my father and get the 'Bonaparte' file transferred . . . before anything happens to it."

Ben and Anita watched their friend leave.

"Good luck," Anita called after him. "We can't stop him, can we?" she added, after the door had closed behind Tom.

"Nope," Ben replied. He hoped his curtness would hide the worry he was really feeling.

"The last one to Telecommunications is a rotten egg!"

"I'm right beside you, lady!"

Five minutes later, the concerned faces of the elder Tom Swift and Gene Larson looked out at them from the telescreen.

"We can't understand you if you're both talking at once," Larson said. He purposely kept the tone of his voice hard and level. It was a successful technique he had acquired through the years for cutting through ambient noise and getting people's attention. It worked on the two excited young people in the *New America* telecom booth who were definitely trying to warn him of something.

" 'Bonaparte!' " Ben shouted at Tom's father and Larson. "Key that sequence from our computer now! It could be wiped at any minute, and that's the proof Tom's been looking for. Grotz's drive doesn't work, and that file tells why."

Ben and Anita watched in tense silence while the two men at Swift Enterprises headquarters concentrated on something out of the telescreen's viewing range—the screen of the giant Langley computer.

Mr. Swift did not take his eyes from the computer screen, but Anita and Ben noted the authority in his voice when he spoke to them, and they listened.

"I'm going to give you some instructions now, and I know they'll be hard for you to follow, but do exactly what I tell you. Do nothing! I know Hans Grotz, and I know what he's capable of!"

"Tom could be in a lot of trouble right now," Anita said.

Ben nodded in worried silence.

"Tom is with Grotz now?" Mr. Swift asked, clearly dismayed.

The two youngsters explained how they had tried to stop him from confronting the acting director.

Mr. Swift turned and issued some rapid orders to someone off-camera. "There is one chance," he said to Ben and Anita, "that we might be able to get to Tom before Grotz tries anything. But we may already be too late!"

Chapter Fifteen

"Let's talk about 'Bonaparte,'" Tom said. He was looking at Grotz from across the acting director's desk. He was unable to see clearly, but he thought the big man flinched almost imperceptibly. Grotz put both hands on the top of his desk and stared at Tom in silence for a few seconds. Then, without warning Grotz lunged at the young man.

Tom was caught completely off guard by Grotz's savage move. He tried to step aside and strike a karate blow at the bigger man, but he was off balance and Grotz was surprisingly agile for his size and age. Grotz came around the desk and struck Tom hard, knocking him down. Then the scientist fell on top of him, deliberately using his weight to knock the breath out of Tom. 157

The boy struggled under the weight of the big man and finally managed to break free, but Grotz was very fast and yanked Tom's feet out from under him. Tom twisted himself around and, for a fraction of a second, saw Grotz's face.

It was red, and the big scientist was sweating heavily from the unaccustomed effort of physically grappling with Tom. But there was no emotion reflected in the man's face. At that moment, Grotz could just as well have been taking the lid off a bottle, hammering a nail, or reading a book, as trying to kill a man.

That's how you could let the passengers and crew of the *Daniel Boone* die without batting an eye, Tom thought. Anita was right. Somewhere on the way up, he had lost his humanity, and never even realized it was gone.

Suddenly, Tom heard the door to Grotz's office open and the sound of footsteps running closer. He looked up to see Chet Worden and Dan Deckert leering down at him. Grotz did not acknowledge their presence; the two thugs must be working for him. That explained a lot of things. Did Anita know?

Grotz continued to strike at Tom with his fist, and now Worden and Deckert joined the fight. Although the young inventor was able to dodge some of the blows, the ones that landed were taking their toll. Tom absorbed more blows, one after the other in painful succession, until a sudden blackness overcame him. He seemed to fall. . . .

Tap, tap, tap-tap, tap . . . click . . . tap, tap, tap-tap.

Tom came to consciousness slowly. He opened his eyes, blinking, his head pounding. He tasted blood. His vision was blurred, and he blinked to bring things into focus.

Everything hurt.

Tom raised his head cautiously and looked in the direction of the sounds. Grotz, alone now, was hunched over a computer terminal, rapidly punching out a series of instructions. Then the big man sat back, watching a screen Tom couldn't see. He murmured in satisfaction and started to rise. Tom quickly feigned unconsciousness again, for he was in no condition to fight, not right then, anyway.

He heard Grotz come toward him, kicking aside some debris from their brief battle. He heard Grotz grunt and then almost gasped aloud as Grotz kicked him. "Fool! You think a kid like you can defeat Hans Grotz?" His laugh was short and nasty. "Now I'll have to take care of your Indian friend, too, you understand!"

Tom heard Grotz walk away, over some broken glass, and then the door closed. Slowly, Tom opened his eyes and sat up, his head swimming. "They must have bounced a few more punches off me when I was out," Tom muttered.

Clinging to the furniture, Tom got to his feet and staggered to the console. He switched to Telecommunications and called Ben's quarters. No response. He tried Anita. Nothing. Then he called Security.

"We can't arrest Doctor Grotz on your say-so, Swift," the young lieutenant said. "He is, after all, acting director." The policeman peered at Tom through the telecom linkage. "You look pretty beat up, man!"

"Never mind that! Find Grotz! Find Ben Walking Eagle!"

"Sorry, man. You come in here, fill out a complaint form, and we'll act on it. But I'm not going to arrest Doctor Grotz on the say-so of any—" Tom heard voices in the background, and then a new face appeared on the screen.

"I'm Sergeant Workman," the man said. "We received an urgent communication from your father, and we were just about to mobilize a search party to find you. Grotz has been spotted at the south end. He's armed, and we think he might be dangerous. We've been unable to locate Benjamin Franklin Walking Eagle—"

"Grotz is after Ben," interrupted Tom. "You've got to find him!"

"We're doing all we can. Your father's on his way up here, too, Son. The best thing for you to do is go to your quarters and stay there until this is all over."

Tom grimaced in irritation. "I can't do that! Grotz intends to kill Ben. And if he finds out Anita Thorwald is involved in this, he'll kill her, too. I've got to find them!"

Tom cut the communication and headed for the door. He paused a moment, then ran back to the computer and punched up Ben's private memory code and asked for a display on 3780, the designation for the Grotz storage.

The screen was blank.

Quickly, Tom checked other codings at random. Grotz had wiped the entire memory core clean. At least Ben and Anita had gotten through to his father. He only hoped that Swift Enterprises had enough information to stop work on the Prometheus drive, because there was no longer any proof—there was nothing. And if Grotz could keep Ben from reconstructing that proof—and that meant killing him—then he would be home free. Who'd believe a couple of teenagers over the great Doctor Hans Friedrich Grotz?

Tom lurched toward the door, his head pounding with every step. Boy, what did they hit me with?

Worden and Deckert! Were they looking for Ben, too? I'd better find Ben before they do, he thought desperately.

Where would Ben and Anita be at this hour, Tom wondered. They weren't home, and they probably weren't at the hangar deck. Ben said he'd installed what he thought was the last improvement on the *Cricket*—a greatly enlarged memory in the on-board computer. He couldn't see Anita and Ben working together because the race was so close. So where were they? We've all been under a lot of tension, maybe they'd relax and—of course! The null-gravity handball court!

Tom stumbled out into the street—every step a painful jolt to his injured head—and an electrocart darted toward him. As it slowed down, Tom recognized Phil Castora, the man he'd met before.

"Phil, please take me to the south end!"

"Hey there, young fella, slow down! I've come to take you to the hospital! Sergeant Workman's orders!"

"No, please, the south end! I've got to stop Doctor Grotz from hurting Ben Walking Eagle! Anita Thorwald might be with him, too!"

"Well, blast!" The old man put out a hand, pulling Tom aboard. "I owe your dad this one. Tell me what happened."

The electrocart gained speed, and Castora wheeled it deftly through the traffic, horn blaring, as Tom outlined the situation.

"Yeah, they're looking for Grotz now, Son," Castora said as he pulled up to the steps at the south end of the colony. "Now I'll just call

Security, and then we'll wait for 'em to meet us here."

But Tom jumped from the electrocart even before it stopped and was going up the steps as fast as he could run. "There's no time for that, Phil," he yelled back.

He stopped for breath and looked up. It was a long, long way, and although he was helped somewhat by the gravity diminishing with each step, it was still a half-mile climb.

Tom started to run again. He concentrated on the steps, three at a time, great leaps. Ignore the pain, he told himself, for it felt as if a spike was driven into his head with each landing.

Run.

Faster.

He stopped again, breathing hard, his stomach heaving from exertion and distress. Our bodies aren't used to weightlessness, he thought. It takes time to adjust, and I'm not giving it time.

Never mind—run!

Suddenly, he realized he had been floating for quite a while, pulling himself along in long, graceful runs. And the aircycle deck was just ahead. Tom veered, going for the spherical shape of the null-gravity court. He grasped a railing and pulled himself up to a window.

Inside two figures were bouncing from wall to wall, leaping back and forth, their arms swinging, sending the ball flying with bewildering speed. Ben and Anita! They were safe!

Tom hurried toward the nearest hatch, and it was then he saw Grotz. The doctor was opening the door, and there was something in his hand—a gun.

It was a needle gun that electrically propelled a small, finned, needlelike projectile. There were a hundred shots in the clip. Grotz was aiming through the hatch.

"Grotz!" Tom yelled.

The gun fired, but Tom's yell had startled him. Grotz fired several more times, almost desperately and without the deliberation of his first shot. He pulled back with a snarl and fired at Tom.

Tom ducked and heard two *pings* off the metal near him. A third shot whistled past his head as Tom wriggled out of sight around the curve of the sphere, along the catwalk.

He grasped a stanchion and pulled himself up a level, getting a quick glimpse through the window there. Anita was floating near a motionless Ben, pulling at the neck of his jumper.

"Hey, Grotz!" Tom called. "It's all over. This won't do any good." His answer was a ricochet an inch from his head. It had come from above; Grotz had sailed over the top, coming at Tom from an unexpected angle.

Tom dodged as another needle rang off the catwalk. The needles did not have the destructive power of a conventional lead bullet, and getting hit by one was not much worse than being injected by an old-fashioned hypodermic needle. But the needles contained a powerful animal tranquilizer that was potent enough to kill a human. Even if the needle gun had conventional-strength projectiles Grotz could dispose of the sleepers as he wished. Eject them into space with suicide notes, send them out in the *Cricket* with empty airtanks, drop them into a fusion torch.

Ping!

Tom knew he had to draw Grotz away. With a hundred shots, he couldn't miss every time. Tom pulled himself frantically along, swinging to the underside of the catwalk, away from Grotz.

Ping! Ponk! Ting!

Grotz wasn't wasting ammunition. He only had two targets—Anita would have to go now, too—and all the rest of a clip.

Pock! Ting!

Tom looked for a weapon as he kept dodging in and out of the grillwork that covered the exterior of the sports sphere. Nothing came in sight; everything was welded down.

The young inventor went over the last railing and toward the rocky hillside below the sphere. Here, as elsewhere all over *New America*, there was a minimum six feet of lunar rock as solar-flare protection. Among the sharp-edged boulders were many small filler rocks. A thin net of plastic fibers had been spread to keep the rocks from floating free in the null-gravity ends, and Tom had a difficult time extracting a fist-sized rock through the netting.

Ponk! Tink! Bonk!

Tom felt a tug at his sleeve and saw a shiny needle imbedded in the tough fabric. He pulled it loose and tossed it away. He tried to get another rock through the netting, but Grotz was following him, growing reckless.

Ping! Whing!

Tom swung around and threw the rock. It struck Grotz in the wrist, and the needle gun dropped from his grasp. Tom dove back for it, swimming through the forest of struts, even as Grotz grasped for it. Tom didn't have time to grab it, only to catch it with his fingers and fling it away with a forceful overhand toss, like a baseball pitcher.

With a roar Grotz grappled with Tom, pummeling him with his fists. The blows were vicious, and there were popping lights in Tom's mind. He broke free, somersaulted away, then propelled himself with his strong legs at the older man. He struck Grotz in the belly, driving him back.

They hit a strut, and Grotz gasped. He struck Tom in the face and kicked free, jumping off toward the top of the sphere. Tom followed, seconds later, seeing Grotz go over the sphere and down toward the aircycle deck.

Tom hesitated. The security people would get Grotz. The needle that had immobilized Ben might be powerful enough to kill him; he'd better get Ben to the hospital.

Tom saw Grotz grab an aircycle and get on, sailing off in a frantic rush, rising into the null-gravity center of the huge city in space. Tom had started to go into the sphere when he realized the fight was not over.

At the far end of *New America* were not only the docking facilities for the shuttles to Earth, but the small-craft dock as well. The racers! Grotz could steal one and get down to Earth, prepare a smoke screen of some sort, deflate or sabotage any attempts to bring him to justice. Suppose Ben couldn't reconstruct what Grotz had destroyed? Suppose Ben were dead? Tom had no proof, none that would stand up in court. Grotz would smother him.

But if he were trapped on *New America,* unable to create a smoke screen . . .

Tom raced for the aircycle deck, pulling himself along in great rushes. He seized a red aircycle and launched himself after Grotz.

He pedaled hard and saw that he was gaining very slowly on the distant figure of the fleeing doctor.

Grotz is a user, Tom thought. He uses people

and casts them aside, and uses them without much regard to their reputations, or lives. He was using *New America* itself as a stepping stone.

I'm gaining, Tom thought.

Grotz looked back and saw Tom. His face contorted into a snarl, and he puffed as he forced the vanes of the aircycle to go faster.

I'm getting out of here, Grotz thought. The people are too idealistic, too convinced that what they are doing is important. They are insignificant *worms,* all of them. What is important is the work I am doing. I'll prove Swift is wrong. I'll claim Swift Enterprises stole and perverted my ideas. *I'll* be the one who will tell the world the *Daniel Boone* is going to blow up. They'll believe me, then!

Tom drew alongside, and Grotz struck out at him. But they were too far apart. In his mad rush to escape, Grotz smashed his aircycle into Tom's. Their vanes crumpled and tore and at once the flimsy vehicles began to break apart, their parts flapping.

Grotz gave a triumphant laugh as he saw Tom's wrecked aircycle falling, slowly picking up speed as the faint gravity tugged at it.

Then he realized he, too, was falling.

Tom kept pumping, hoping the wrecked vanes would slow his descent. It was a half mile down from this point—and he had no parachute!

Chapter Sixteen

Tom had done a little skydiving back on Earth. The worst moment was always stepping out. The falling itself was the best part. It was like flying, with little sensation of falling, at least in the higher altitudes. You spread your arms and legs and sailed. You could roll into a ball and drop faster, and you could angle a bit for minor course corrections.

But as you got closer to the ground, it felt more like falling, and it was then you opened your chute, and it was then you hoped it would open.

But Tom had no parachute.

From the corner of his eye, Tom saw the flailing figure of Hans Grotz. Far below, plummeting down in ragged, flopping fashion, was the wreckage of the older man's aircycle. Tom saw something hit the surface of the lake and . . .

The lake!

The artificial gravity caused by the rotation of *New America* was not quite full Earth gravity, but it was close, close enough to kill a man if he fell far enough onto the hard surface of the cylinder.

But not, maybe, if he splashed.

Tom calculated the angle at which he was falling. Would he come down into the water or hit the houses clustered along that side?

In a sense, Tom was amazed at his own calm. He was not panicking. Long ago, his father had told him that when there was a cause for panic that was the worst time to panic, and Tom had found his advice to be good.

Tom could see that he wasn't going to make it into the lake, not by some yards. He was headed right into the thin-walled cluster of houses surrounding a mossy Oriental-style garden. But he would try.

He kept pumping the damaged aircycle, and he spread out his arms, offering as much resistance to the air as possible. He tilted his body, letting air slip to the right, sending his body to the left, toward the blue water.

How deep was it? It didn't matter. It was all he had.

Closer . . .

Very fast . . .

At the last minute, Tom pushed the aircycle from him and rolled into a ball, tucking his face into his raised knees and grasping his ankles.

He hit.

It felt as if he had hit cement—a powerful blow over his entire body. Roaring sound. Water engulfed him. Then blackness.

"Tom!"

He became aware of pain. He felt pummeled and beaten.

"Tom! Wake up!"

He groaned and heard someone cry out, "He's coming round!"

Tom opened his eyes and saw two Bens. He blinked and focused and there was only one. "Ben—"

"Thank heavens, you're safe!" The words poured out of Ben. "Some security men saw you two fall, you and Doctor Grotz, so they got to you right away! Artificial breathing, they made you breathe again! You were out, really out, Tom, thank heavens you weren't killed." Ben leaned over his friend. "What were you doing up there? They said you ran into Grotz and—"

Tom waved a hand weakly. "Hold it. What happened to Grotz?"

Ben pointed away, and Tom became aware of a ring of anxious faces. "He fell into a house. Right through it, actually. He's all busted up, but he'll live, they say. The house kind of collapsed under him, like the cardboard boxes stunt men use in movies. They think they're going to have to replace his legs, but we'll know soon. Listen, never mind him, it's you we're worrying about and—"

The white-suited emergency-services people crowded through and set down a stretcher. "Move back, please. Give us room," one of them said. He began at once to examine Tom.

"I'm all right," Tom said. "Bruised a little, but I'm all right."

"You're going to the hospital, fella," the attendant said.

"The race, I've got to get into the race."

"Forget it, they've all left," the attendant muttered, opening Tom's drenched tunic and looking at his bruises.

"Tom, forget the race," Ben said.

"No," Tom said, struggling to get up.

The attendant looked at his partner. "Possible concussion?" The other one shrugged and held out a shiny instrument. Tom tried to get away from it, but the medic was too quick. It felt cold against his chest, and there was a hissing.

Once again, the world collapsed into blackness.

He came out of it slowly, aware of faint clicks and distant hums. It was white and beige. A hospital room.

"Well, welcome back!" a woman said. The nurse came to the side of his bed, smiling, holding a chart.

Tom blinked and asked, "How long was I out?"

The nurse looked at the chart, then at her wrist communicator. "Almost two hours. They've checked you over—no concussion, nothing broken. You were pretty lucky. We had one woman go into the lake a few months ago and they have still got her plugged into machines."

"I've got to get up and—"

"Oh, no, you don't, Mister Swift! You must stay right here for a few days. They want to look you over some more. Don't you worry. Doctor Massolia is the best we have on things like this." The nurse fussed with the covers. "Your friend, Ben, the Indian fella? He said you were supposed to be in some race, but you just get some sleep now. There will be other races." She patted him and left the room.

Carefully Tom sat up. He had a slight headache and he felt as if he had been beaten with rubber hoses. He hurt all over.

But he grinned—I'm alive! His thoughts were triumphant as he carefully lowered himself to the floor. There was no closet, only a door and a long window.

Tom went to the window and dialed a section of it from translucent to transparent and looked out. He was on the lower slopes of the south end, which accounted for the slight lessening of gravity he felt. But the window didn't open.

He went to the door and looked out, cautiously. Just outside a laundry hamper was parked. Tom could see two nurse's aides changing sheets across the hall. He noticed a robe wadded up in the hamper and reached in and got it.

There were slippers under his bed, and he put them on as he belted the robe. Acting casual, but moving slowly, Tom left the room and went down the hall. There were some nurses talking in the corridor ahead, so he went into a side corridor, smiled at another nurse, and opened a door marked FIRE EXIT.

It was only one floor down, and the door to the outside opened easily. The racing-ship dock was overhead at the center of the domed end. A few people looked oddly at him as he trotted along, but said nothing.

He was almost four hours past his starting time. He was racing the clock and starting with a negative time factor. In the locker room next to the landing-dock airlock, he punched out the code on his locker and took out his spacesuit.

Tom Swift was in the seat of his racer, going quickly over the preflight list, when he heard a familiar voice in his suit radio.

"Going to kill yourself, huh?"

"Hi, Ben. No, listen, I'm all right, really."

"You drop into a lake and tell me you're all right? Going to win the race all busted up?"

"They checked me out, I'm okay. Where are you?"

"Cycling through the airlock and ..." The lock opened, and Ben came out, moving slowly. "Here I am." He carried a big tank of oxygen under each arm, tugging the mass along with his magnetic shoes on the metal flooring.

"What do you think you're doing?" Tom asked.

"Going with you. I'm your copilot, remember?"

"Ben—"

"Grab the end of that, will you? You will notice I added a few things—extra food-pellet bins, that water tank there, some music tapes."

"Music tapes?" Tom asked.

"Put that end right in there, that's it. Sure, music. Bagpipe solos, "Concerto for Oompah and Tin Can," the Cleveland Marching Band and Egg-Rolling Society, *The 1812 Overture* done by the Santa Rosa Grammar School Timpani Band, the—"

"Okay, okay—enough!" The airtanks were

strapped down and the two friends clambered into the tiny cabin of radiation shielding. They sealed the chamber and finished the preflight check. They backed out of the dock on the airjets and turned the ship, moving slowly away from *New America* to a distance suitable for starting up the powerful fusion drive.

"*New America* Control, this is *Davy Cricket*, ready to begin flight. Please give me the countdown."

"*Davy Cricket*, you're running pretty late. Why bother?"

Ben broke in. "Hey, Marty, just start timing, okay?"

"You got it, *Cricket*. Ten seconds on my mark . . . now!"

Tom looked at Ben and gave him a thumbs-up gesture, which Ben repeated. The clock ticked over. On automatic sequence, the fusion drive burst into life, and the *Davy Cricket* began to move.

New America dropped away. The stars turned and steadied, as the small craft raced toward *Sunflower*.

Tom took off his helmet, Ben unlatched his, and they hung them up. "Bagpipe music?" Tom asked incredulously.

"Oh, sure," Ben said, waving his hand airily. "You should hear the way they do Paul McCartney! Absolutely inspiring!"

Tom looked at his friend, expressionless. "Well, you know what they say—there's no accounting for taste!"

On the final approach to rendezvous with *Sunflower*, they were told they had gained eighty-seven minutes on the leader. It was no surprise that the leader was Anita Thorwald's *Valkyrie*. They still had a long way to go and were hours behind.

They saw the *Régine* in a docking bay, along with the *Marjii Ellers*, the *Lizzy L*, the *Moonstreak*, and the *Rothstein Special*. They had caught up to the tail-enders—and to Worden and Deckert. The fact that the two creeps were still in the race meant that they had figured Tom would not make it and that their association with Grotz was still a secret. They were in for a big surprise.

"Let's make this as fast as possible," Tom said as they stretched wearily in the locker room. He felt battered and stiff.

The *Sunflower* colony was arranged differently from *New America*; the racers had docked in the hub that pierced the doughnut of the living and working quarters. Now Tom and Ben went quickly along the hub to a shower area, arranged especially for use during the race, then to a dining room.

They found some other racers just getting ready to leave, finishing up their meals. Worden and Deckert were nowhere in sight. Tom and Ben spotted Bernie Rothstein sitting moodily in a corner, and took their trays over.

"Hi, Bernie," Ben said, putting his plate down next to him.

"Hello." Rothstein looked at Tom and Ben with hooded, tired eyes. "I've quit. No way I can catch up. Tom, your ship is the only one that can catch *Valkyrie*. Yours and maybe the *Elie Metchnikoff*. The rest are just wasting time. I'm afraid the day of the ion rocket is over, just like that of the chemical rocket and the internal-combustion engine. I'm finished. I'm only at *Sunflower* and I was second to start!"

"Hang in there, Bernie. A lot of things can happen," offered Ben. "People drop out, ships fail . . ."

Bernie shook his head. "There are only three fusion ships. The rest of us are just extras in this play. Fillers. We're trying to see who is fourth, that's all." He poked gloomily at his plate of half-consumed food. "*The Elie Metchnikoff* is the slowest. He's using a very old principle, and he has some navigation problems. Thorwald's good; her fusion plant is powerful, but her control is not exactly perfect. They said she overshot *Sunflower* and had to make a second pass. No, it's among you three."

The short, chubby young man pointed his fork at Tom. "Just before the start of the race, we all heard what happened with you and Grotz. There are some other rumors going around, too. I'd watch it, if I were you, naming no names."

"You mean Worden and Deckert?" Ben said, but Rothstein refused to respond. Ben and Tom exchanged looks, then quickly bolted from the dining room and ran for their ship!

Chapter Seventeen

The two young racers spent several minutes searching for any indication of sabotage to the *Davy Cricket* but everything seemed to be just as they had left it. Ben ran a computer check and it also indicated that all was well.

By the time they had strapped down in the tiny, shielded cabin and locked the magnetic grapple, all but one racer, the *Marjii Ellers,* had left.

"Next stop—the Moon," Tom said.

Armstrong Base was a sprawling complex in the fifty-mile crater of Daedalus, on the dark side of the Moon. Here, in the second of America's outposts on the Moon, were the largest of the observatories and the extensive mining operations that not only supplied *New America* and *Sunflower* with essential materials, but Earth as well.

The rules of the race required a complete touchdown and shutdown within a prescribed area assigned to each ship. Tom set the *Davy Cricket* down carefully. This was, after all, the fragile craft's first real contact with gravity.

While the Moon had only one-sixth the gravity of Earth, it was still gravity. The Earth-Moon system was considered a double-planet system by some, because the Moon's mass was $\frac{1}{81}$ that of Earth's; the satellites of all the other planets had only a few thousandths the mass of their mother worlds.

The welded tubular construction of the *Cricket* survived, and Tom and Ben walked across the scratched and pitted crater floor to the control bunker in the slow-motion dance common on the Moon.

Inside they found corridors cut by lasers and sealed with transparent plastic. Big mining machines with self-contained living quarters were parked in bays next to the equipment airlock. Ingots from the solar-powered smelters were piled on docks ready to be shipped to the mass accelerator. People wearing jumpers and dungarees operated cranes and electrocarts. A big all-purpose carrier rumbled by with a huge tank of oxygen retrieved from rocks that had been ripped into atoms by fusion torches.

"You're only sixty-one minutes behind Thorwald," one of the other racers said wryly. "What kind of pusher you got on that crate, anyway, Swift?"

"A bagpipe," Tom said. "Ben plays these tapes, and we try to outrun the noise."

"Where's food?" Ben grumbled. He moved stiffly over to a table in the room and sat down. "This makes more than three days sitting in the same position," he grumbled. "I feel as though I've been riveted into this shape."

"Eat," Tom said.

"Drink and be merry, I know," Ben muttered. "Waiter!"

The longest leg of the race was from Armstrong Base, around the Moon, and to the L-5 spot where *New America* was "moored" by the gravitational tides. The sight of Earth as they came up over the rim of the Moon was still exciting to the young men.

Tom and Ben had both grown up with the photograph of Earth, as seen from space, as an almost daily reminder, but its glamour and interest had never waned for either of them. It was still their true symbol of space. Not the Moon, not the stars, but Earth, blue and white and tan, without a single sign of civilization showing until you were nearly down through the atmosphere. From out in space it looked unpolluted, still fresh.

But it wasn't, and that was the very best argument for the establishment of cities in space, of moving out to explore the other worlds around them, and then—in time, with luck and diligence—the stars.

"*Cricket,* this is *New America* Control."

"Go ahead, Control," Tom said.

"Phil Castora wants to talk to you, Swift."

"Roger."

"Hey, Tom!" The man who had befriended Tom was cackling with pleasure. "Thought you'd want to know. Greg Ellison came out of it okay. Got a lot of new parts. They had to give him a section of artificial spinal cord sheathing, and a couple of spare bits of innards, but he's alive, awake, and waiting to thank you."

"That's great, Phil!" Tom grinned at Ben, who gave him a thumbs-up signal.

"And another thing, Tom. Our great and un-lamented ex–acting director, Doctor H. F. Grotz, is gonna live. Rats!" Phil laughed again. "Course, he's getting a new set of metal legs, just as soon as he gets better. Heard he wanted to be made two inches taller."

"That sounds like him," Ben muttered.

"Course, at the trial, he won't have a leg to stand on! Greg'll testify, and there's the computer records. He pretty near got the whole *Dan'l Boone* blown up!"

"I'm afraid so, Phil. You tell Greg to take it easy, and we'll be seeing him soon," Tom said.

"Betcha. Y'know, boy, I hate to say this, 'specially over an open line like this, but there's been some bettin' on you hereabouts." Castora chuckled again. "Not everyone thought you had such a fast ship, y'know."

"Hey, Phil," Ben said. "You going to get rich?"

"Only if you two rascals get back here first!"

"We'll do our best," Tom promised.

"By the way," Castora cackled, "you boys may be interested to know that the *Régine* dropped out of the race right after *Sunflower*. They just launched and then flew off the course and headed for parts unknown."

Ben looked at Tom meaningfully. "You were right, Tom, they didn't figure on you being around to testify against them. I guess they didn't want to go down the tube with Grotz!"

"Okay, boys, you play it right, now, hear?"

Castora signed off, and Ben and Tom settled back in their seats. One thing that hadn't become routine from all the traveling they'd done in space was the stars. Tom had not really realized how colorful they were. From Earth they all seemed much the same, their light filtered through the blanket of atmosphere. But out here you could see all their myriad colors, and Tom thought he could even detect shadings in the dots of distant light.

He shifted uncomfortably in his bucket seat. His bruises were almost gone. Both he and Ben had taken turns "exercising" on the ends of tethers as they raced along, but he was tired, sore, sick of food pellets, and very stiff. He and Ben had told each other the stories of their lives, or so it seemed, and had played hours of computer games together and with the crew of the *Moonglow*, whom they had overtaken and passed.

But the end was near. They had passed the *Queen of Mars* less than an hour before, exchanging amiable insults with the crew from the Los Angeles Space Yacht Club. Within a few minutes they would pass the *Moonstreak*, then the *Vespucci* and the *Martian Flash*. The emergency band had already announced that both the *Hobbit* and one of the Russian racers had developed trouble and dropped out. Tugs were coming out to get them.

Tom and Ben had been flying out, with only two stops, for five days. The *Minerva*, the *Elie Metchnikoff*, and the *Valkyrie* were ahead, and still going strong.

"That you, *Cricket?*" came a voice from the radio. "This is *Moonstreak*. You guys are coming up our tail pretty fast."

"*Moonstreak*, this is *Davy Cricket*," Ben responded. "How about moving over, slowpokes?"

"Ben, that you? I thought Swift had the *Cricket*."

"Hi, Maureen. Tom and I are riding double. This is the hottest ship in the race. Make way for the winner!"

"Not over yet, Ben." Another female voice laughed.

"Hey, Leigh, you are riding yesterday's ship. This is the ship of the future, guys!"

"Uh-huh," Maureen said doubtfully. "If you jokers are going to blow up, please don't get too close, huh?"

Tom broke in. "We're safe this time." They continued to chat as the two ships got closer and closer. Then the *Cricket* was ahead, and Maureen was making wry comments about the tortoise and the hare.

They streaked past the drifting *Hobbit* and shortly after that the radar showed the *Peter the Great* off to lower starboard. The bulbous *Vespucci* was next. They were slowly gaining on the swift ion-drive *Martian Flash*, the entry from Britain. But it, too, fell behind the hard-driving *Cricket.*

Ben bent over the radar screen and punched out a recognition signal. Each space vehicle had a distinctive digital code that was triggered by a radar sweep. The vessel's transponder read as clearly as if they had seen it lettered on the stern of a wooden sailing ship, *Minerva.*

They swept past the sleek, fully shielded vessel. Instead of voice contact, the pilot sent them a diagram on their screen, one which corresponded to the ancient maritime signal "Acknowledge your passage."

Tom and Ben exchanged grins, for they were filled with delight. The *Minerva* had been an early leader, and now, even with their late start, they were passing the hot, blue-white flare of the ion-driven ship.

The *Elie Metchnikoff* was ahead. Named after the late nineteenth-century bacteriologist and zoologist who developed the theory that certain white corpuscles ingest and destroy bacteria, the craft was piloted by Dale Bailey, a tall, slender biologist living on *New America.* The space colony itself was on the radar screen as a distant dot as they passed him.

Only the *Valkyrie* was ahead, another radar dot closing fast.

Tom and Ben shot past a news-agency ship and a number of partying well-wishers in small tuglike vessels. Then Tom turned the ship over to begin the descent to the landing deck of *New America,* the flaming jet acting as a brake to their headlong flight.

The *Valkyrie* was just ahead, off to their starboard, as the *Cricket* came down, its fusion torch bright. Anita cut her drive first, but Tom kept theirs going, slowing the *Cricket* even more. Ben monitored both their approach and Anita's.

It was going to be close.

"Hey!" Ben said suddenly. "I don't think she's going to dock right, she's—uh-oh!"

"What?" demanded Tom, who was watching the readouts closely. He wanted no possibility of any damage to *New America* or to his own racer and its crew. He'd rather lose the race.

"She got too eager. She's . . . she's veering off!" Ben stared at the distant dot. "She came in too fast and wasn't right. She's got to come around again—just like they said at *Sunflower*! Tom, we've won!"

"We've won if we don't have to go around again, too," Tom responded. His face was taut with concentration. This was the fastest approach he had ever dared make. It was not something he had practiced. Under ideal conditions, you use the fusion drive to slow down, then, calculating just what you need, cut it off and drift in.

That was the ideal. This was a race. Already he could see the *Metchnikoff* coming down on a long streak of flame. Anita was turning her craft, slower now, moving into position.

There was always the danger of collision. Tom could hear the excited, cautionary words from

New America Control, but he ignored them. Things were happening too fast. The docking deck was coming up fast. Everything was happening too quickly for talk.

"Now!" Tom snapped, and Ben fired the magnetic grapples to the deck. The racer drifted past the deck, then came to a halt as the cables cushioned their stop. Ben reeled them in.

They were back.

They had won.

Anita Thorwald smiled ruefully at Tom. Mark Scott, who had been her copilot, shook their hands. "Okay, here," Anita said, sticking out her hand. "I blew it by rushing it."

"We had you beat on time, anyway," Ben grinned.

Anita gave Ben a dark look. "Go on, rub it in. Whatever happened to generous winners?"

They were on a small stage under bright lights with cameras aimed at them from almost every angle. "Shake hands again," someone shouted. Mark stuck out his hand once more and Tom took it. They all turned as Dale Bailey, the pilot of the *Elie Metchnikoff,* entered. He had placed third.

Once again, there was a round of handshaking, then Tom and Ben were called forward, but Ben pushed Tom out ahead. "Hey, I was just a passenger, really. This is your show, Tom."

Tom took a deep breath and approached the microphones. "I want to congratulate my fellow racers for running a good race." There were scattered cheers. "And a special thanks to Benjamin Franklin Walking Eagle—my copilot!" He drew Ben forward to more cheers and applause, and Ben grinned widely.

When the applause had died down, Tom spoke again, this time more seriously. "We'll go see the worlds in our solar system—the worlds that only a generation or so ago they were saying we'd never visit. In our own galaxy, there are an estimated six hundred forty million *Earth-type* planets. Planets so much like ours you could step out of the airlock, take a deep breath, and look up at a blue sky.

"We are barely off the surface of our home planet. Barely. We only got this far by sheerest luck. But Earth is just too small and far too fragile for us to keep humanity confined to it. What we are doing is searching infinity, stretching the spirit of mankind to the utmost.

"There may be life out there, intelligent life. It seems almost certain, mathematically. We don't know. But isn't it better to go see than to wait around until maybe they come this way?

"We have broken free from the chains that bound us to Earth. From 'Spaceship Earth' to starships we will advance." Suddenly Tom was embarrassed. He hadn't meant to make a speech, but the exploration of space was so important to him he had been carried away. "Thank you," he said, and stepped back, only to see his father, standing proudly next to him. The two of them shook hands and embraced, then stepped down from the stage. Tom brought his father to meet his friends.

"Dad, this is Ben Walking Eagle."

The tall man offered his hand to Ben. "Congratulations, Ben!"

"Anita, Dale, Mark—meet my father."

Introductions were made. Interviews were held. The official presentation was made to the winners.

It took hours, but then finally Tom Swift was alone. He walked away from the partying crowd and leaned on a wall overlooking one of *New America*'s huge windows. Outside Tom could see stars in that spilling path called the Milky Way.

The sky was so full of planets, of stars, of galaxies. There seemed no boundaries to the universe.

Little did Tom realize how soon he and his friends would be up there, making one of the greatest scientific discoveries in the history of mankind—and fighting for their lives—in *Tom Swift: Terror on the Moons of Jupiter*.

Tom sighed and started walking to the quarters he shared with Ben. One step at a time, Tom thought. One small step at a time.

THE TOM SWIFT® SERIES
by Victor Appleton

The City in the Stars (#1)
Terror on the Moons of Jupiter (#2)
The Alien Probe (#3)
The War in Outer Space (#4)

You will also enjoy
THE HARDY BOYS® MYSTERY STORIES
by Franklin W. Dixon

Night of the Werewolf (#59)
Mystery of the Samurai Sword (#60)
The Pentagon Spy (#61)
The Apeman's Secret (#62)
The Mummy Case (#63)
Mystery of Smugglers Cove (#64)
The Stone Idol (#65)
The Vanishing Thieves (#66)